Discover the world
in the critically ac...

EDGAR AWARD-NOMINATED AUTHOR

JOHN R. RIGGS

. . . and don't miss any of these
"PAGE TURNERS"

The Drood Review of Mystery

MacGregor's Book
Nook Discard
202 North Main Street
Yreka, CA 96097
(530) 841-2664

HUNTING GROUND

Cheerleader, homecoming queen, the girl most likely . . . to
die. What secrets does Oakalla know about the most
popular girl in high school?

HAUNT OF THE NIGHTINGALE

The blonde stranger hiding out in Garth's barn doesn't
speak a word—but sings a mysterious song of murder . . .

WOLF IN SHEEP'S CLOTHING

Old loves never really die, and Garth's heart—and his
life—are up for grabs when his former lover disappears.

ONE MAN'S POISON

Cyanide in the water supply. A missing father and son.
The untimely death of the local judge. Sometimes small town
life can be murder . . .

THE LAST LAUGH

When the town prankster dies, Garth finds
that someone has a killing sense of humor . . .

LET SLEEPING DOGS LIE

A vintage car is the key to
a murder from another era . . .

MORE MYSTERIES FROM THE
BERKLEY PUBLISHING GROUP . . .

INSPECTOR KENWORTHY MYSTERIES: Scotland Yard's consummate master of investigation lets no one get away with murder. "In the best tradition of British detective fiction!" —*Boston Globe*

by John Buxton Hilton

HANGMAN'S TIDE	TARGET OF SUSPICION
FATAL CURTAIN	TWICE DEAD
PLAYGROUND OF DEATH	RANSOM GAME
CRADLE OF CRIME	FOCUS ON CRIME
HOLIDAY FOR MURDER	CORRIDORS OF GUILT
LESSON IN MURDER	DEAD MAN'S PATH

DOG LOVER'S MYSTERIES STARRING JACKIE WALSH: She's starting a new life with her son and an ex-police dog named Jake . . . teaching film classes and solving crimes!

by Melissa Cleary

A TAIL OF TWO MURDERS	HOUNDED TO DEATH
DOG COLLAR CRIME	SKULL AND DOG BONES

GARTH RYLAND MYSTERIES: Newsman Garth Ryland digs up the dirt in a serene small town—that isn't as peaceful as it looks . . . "A writer with real imagination!" —*The New York Times*

by John R. Riggs

HUNTING GROUND	ONE MAN'S POISON
HAUNT OF THE NIGHTINGALE	THE LAST LAUGH
WOLF IN SHEEP'S CLOTHING	LET SLEEPING DOGS LIE

PETER BRICHTER MYSTERIES: A midwestern police detective stars in "a highly unusual, exceptionally erudite mystery series!" —*Minneapolis Star Tribune*

by Mary Monica Pulver

KNIGHT FALL	ORIGINAL SIN
THE UNFORGIVING MINUTES	SHOW STOPPER
ASHES TO ASHES	

JACK HAGEE, P.I., MYSTERIES: Classic detective fiction with "raw vitality . . . Henderson is a born storyteller." —*Armchair Detective*

by C.J. Henderson

NO FREE LUNCH	SOMETHING FOR NOTHING

FREDDIE O'NEAL, P.I., MYSTERIES: You can bet that this appealing Reno P.I. will get her man . . . "A winner." —*Linda Grant*

by Catherine Dain

LAY IT ON THE LINE	SING A SONG OF DEATH

DEAD LETTER

JOHN R. RIGGS

JOVE BOOKS, NEW YORK

If you purchased this book without a cover, you should be aware that this book is stolen property. It was reported as "unsold and destroyed" to the publisher, and neither the author nor the publisher has received any payment for this "stripped book."

This Jove Book contains the complete
text of the original edition.
It has been completely reset in a typeface
designed for easy reading and was printed
from new film.

DEAD LETTER

A Jove Book / published by arrangement with
Barricade Books

PRINTING HISTORY
Barricade edition published 1992
Jove edition / January 1994

All rights reserved.
Copyright © 1992 by John R. Riggs.
This book may not be reproduced in whole
or in part, by mimeograph or any other means,
without permission. For information address:
Barricade Books, 61 Fourth Avenue,
New York, New York 10003.

ISBN: 0-515-11280-1

A JOVE BOOK®
Jove Books are published by The Berkley Publishing Group,
200 Madison Avenue, New York, New York 10016.
JOVE and the "J" design
are trademarks belonging to Jove Publications, Inc.

PRINTED IN THE UNITED STATES OF AMERICA

10 9 8 7 6 5 4 3 2 1

To Mulberry, my hometown; Greencastle, my home;
and as always, to Carole.

AMEL PILKIN WAS as deaf as a post. But he could read your lips if you spoke slowly and carefully and kept your face directly toward him. And he could make himself understood if he took the time to try, and you had the patience to listen. However, on that Friday night in the Corner Bar and Grill, neither Amel nor I was doing a very good job of communicating.

Ruth and I sat at a booth in the northwest corner of the barroom. Amel Pilkin sat at the bar, wearing a red plaid sport coat several sizes too big for him and the look of man who had just won the lottery. He was talking to me now, as he had been for the past five minutes, but I had yet to understand a word he'd said. I'd wait until he finished each monologue, smile when he'd smile, laugh when he'd laugh, then feign interest whenever he'd start up again. Meanwhile my stomach began to growl and my supper got cold.

Amel reached inside his sport coat and withdrew a white envelope, which he waved at me as he hugged himself in glee. I smiled at him as if I knew what was going on. That was all the encouragement he needed. He began to talk to me in rapid-fire utterances, laughing and gesturing as he did.

Amel Pilkin stood no more than four feet ten inches tall. He had thick, dark-blond, wavy hair, short stubby arms and legs, and an unusually large head for someone his size. He reminded me of a squirrel, who sat there on the barstool barking at me, as his head jerked to a rhythm of his words. And he might as well have been a squirrel for all the sense he made.

Then without warning and apparently right in mid-sentence, Amel jumped from the barstool, squared his shoulders, and started for the stairway that led down to the basement and the restrooms therein. Despite his small stature, Amel always walked straight and proud, like the cock of the walk. I couldn't help but smile at him. When I turned to look at Ruth, I noticed she was smiling, too.

A moment after Amel disappeared down the stairs, newly elected sheriff, Whitey Huffer, came into the barroom, stood a moment to look things over, and left without saying a word. With a sigh of relief, I dug my fork into my catfish and began to eat.

The reason that Ruth and I were at the Corner Bar and Grill on a cold Friday night in mid-November was that I owed her a supper. We'd bet on the Bears-Packers game and I'd lost. As always, she'd taken the Packers. As always, I'd taken the Bears. I thought it was a safe bet at the time.

"Do you have any idea what Amel was talking about?" I asked, while trying to stuff down as much catfish as I could before he came back.

Ruth Krammes and I had been together for eleven years, ever since I moved to Oakalla, Wisconsin, and advertised in the *Oakalla Reporter*, my then-fledgling weekly newspaper, for a live-in housekeeper. Ruth, who had some thirty years on me, was now in her early seventies, though she didn't look it, and had an imperious frown, steel-grey hair, and shoulders broad enough to carry the weight of whatever you wanted to pack on them, including me. Over the years we'd forged a friendship that had never needed to prove itself. I knew I could count on her. She knew she could count on me. That was all we needed to know.

"No," she said. "I couldn't understand a word Amel said. But whatever he was talking about, he was surely excited about it."

Sheriff Whitey Huffer came back into the barroom for another look around. This time he saw me sitting there in the corner booth. That brought a scowl to his face.

Rupert Roberts, my good friend and mentor, had decided not to run for a fourth term as sheriff of Adams County, Wisconsin. The reason he gave was that he had been sheriff longer than anyone else in the history of Adams County, and he felt that a change was needed for his own good and the good of the county. The real reason, the one he didn't talk about, was that his wife, Elvira, had been after him for years to slow down, and after a near heart attack, he finally had decided to listen to her.

In the election, now ten days old, Chief Deputy Harold Clark, or Clarkie as we in Oakalla knew him, had run against Whitey Huffer and lost by four votes. Out of loyalty to Clarkie and a sincere belief that he was the best man for the job, I had put myself and the *Oakalla Reporter* solidly behind him. So Clarkie's loss was a defeat for both him and me and a victory for Whitey Huffer.

"I didn't think you'd have the guts to show your face in public again," Whitey Huffer said to me. "Especially after what you said about me in that newspaper of yours."

"Aside from the fact that you had no track record in law enforcement and no real roots in Adams County, what else did I say about you?" I said.

"That was enough," he said, "to let everyone know whose side you were on."

I took a bite of cold catfish and washed it down with a swallow of warm beer. "I thought that was obvious from the beginning."

Whitey Huffer was about six feet tall with hard eyes and soft hands, prematurely white hair, and a penchant for leather jackets, leather gloves, and leather cowboy boots. Though not a farmer or anything remotely resembling one, he lived on the largest farm in Adams County, just south of Oakalla, and up until the election had worked as a security guard for a bank in Madison. Personally I had nothing against him since our paths had rarely crossed until recently, but I couldn't say that I ever had liked the way he went about things. I also resented the fact that he was married to Claire Huffer, one of the few women I coveted.

Whitey Huffer stared at me, trying to stare me down. I looked at my catfish. Had I eaten all that I wanted? I guessed so.

"Was there something you wanted?" I asked, shoving my plate aside.

"Not from you," he said. "Not unless you're offering an apology."

"For what?"

"Saying what you said about me."

"What I said about you was the truth, Whitey. Don't ask me to apologize for it."

I felt Ruth kick me under the table, but I ignored her. I hated to lose at anything, and I particularly hated to lose the election to Whitey Huffer. If I had the next fifty years or so, maybe then I'd get over it.

"You said I had no roots in Adams County. That's a lie, Ryland. Acre for acre I have more roots than anybody else."

"You married the land, Whitey," I said. "You weren't raised on it."

"What's that supposed to mean?" He took a step toward me.

"Forget it," I said. "You won the election in spite of me. So that should make us even."

He made his gloved hand into a fist and held it up for me and everyone else in the barroom to see. "When I've planted this in your face, that's when we'll be even, Ryland. Not before." He wheeled and left the barroom as abruptly as he came.

"I guess you told him, Garth," Ruth said.

"What did you want me to do," I said, "challenge him to a duel at sunrise?"

"You might try keeping your mouth shut next time. And leave well enough alone."

As I drank the last of my beer, I noticed my hand shook with anger. "If he'll leave me alone."

Ruth ordered blueberry pie and coffee for dessert—to get her money's worth, she said. I sat there nursing my hurt pride and wondering where Amel Pilken had gone. He'd left his trash-collection route book and a wad of money on the bar, neither of which he could afford to lose.

"I wonder what happened to Amel," I finally thought aloud to Ruth. "He should be back by now."

"I don't know. How long has he been gone?"

"Too long for me not to wonder."

I slid out of the booth and went down the stairs to the men's restroom. Amel wasn't in there. Neither was he in the women's restroom, the wine cellar, or anywhere else in the basement that I could see.

That didn't mean that Amel had disappeared into thin air. You could go all the way from the basement of the Corner Bar and Grill to the basement of the hardware by going through the basement under Sniffy Smith's barbershop. But I hated to make that journey in the dark.

"Find him?" Ruth asked when I returned to our booth.

"No."

She had finished her blueberry pie and laid what was left of the crust on top the catfish bones. "That's not like Amel to just pick up and leave like that," she said. "Or leave his route book behind."

"Right on both counts," I said.

"So what do you think got into him?"

"How should I know, Ruth? You were sitting here the same as me."

"But I'm not the one Amel was talking to."

"Jabbering, Ruth," I said, irritated by the way the evening had gone, which was a far cry from the quiet, thank-God-it's-Friday, peaceful evening I'd envisioned. "He was talking a mile a minute. I couldn't begin to understand him."

"Even if you'd tried," she said.

"Are you ready to go?"

"Yes."

"Then let's do it."

I went to the bar to pay the bill. Hiram, the bartender, met me with a frown on his face. "You have any idea where Amel went?" he asked.

"No. Ruth and I were just wondering the same thing."

He picked up the wad of money from the bar and counted it. "There's close to twenty dollars here. Amel never leaves that kind of money laying around."

"I know that."

"So what do you suppose got into the little monkey?" he asked.

"I don't know. Maybe he had too much to drink."

Hiram shook his head at that suggestion. "I don't hardly see how. One's all that Amel had. " He looked down at Amel's glass, which was about half full. "And he didn't even drink all of that."

"What about before he came in here?" I asked.

"I don't think he'd been drinking. At least not so I could tell." He smiled. "And with Amel you can usually tell."

I returned his smile. With Amel you usually could tell what was what, even when you couldn't understand him. Amel Pilkin had the most expressive hands and face of anyone I'd ever known.

I picked up Amel's route book and handed it to Hiram. "You might as well put this in a safe place. Amel's going to be in here first thing in the morning, looking for it."

"I'll leave a note to Bernice to see that he gets it." He held up the wad of one-dollar bills. "Along with these."

Ruth and I left by the side door of the Corner Bar and Grill, so I could see if Amel's old yellow Toyota pickup was still parked in front of the hardware, where I'd last seen it a couple hours earlier. But the pickup was gone.

"Well, he's gone somewhere," I said to Ruth. "He must have come out the front door of the hardware and taken off."

"It looks like it," she said.

"Where do you think he went?"

She turned away from the cold west wind and put both hands in her coat pockets. "He went home if he had any sense. Which is where I'm going."

She left for home. I soon caught up to her. We walked together the rest of the way.

2

THE NEXT MORNING I sat in my office at the *Oakalla Reporter* with my stocking cap on, a space heater at my feet, a sweatshirt over my flannel shirt, and a hot cup of coffee in my hand. Still I was cold.

Dawn had been slow in coming. Black had turned to dark grey, as the trees across Gas Line Road gradually took shape, and the sparrows in the bush outside my window began to chirp. Dark grey had turned to light grey and held there, as the cars that came and went along Gas Line Road kept their lights on, and the streetlight on the corner did the same. It was a sleepy morning. A lazy morning. A perfect morning to sit inside and do absolutely nothing.

A red Buick Regal with a car carrier on top and a trailer on behind pulled up outside. Rupert Roberts got out of the Buick and came into my office. He stood there a moment, as if unsure of himself, before taking his old familiar seat just inside the door. As usual, his cheek bulged with a chew of tobacco. I got up, rummaged through my wastebasket, then handed him an empty Coke can to spit in.

"Much obliged," he said.

Lean and lanky, with large hands, a large heart, and large somber bloodhound eyes, Rupert Roberts was the only three-term sheriff in the history of Adams County. Or at least he was sheriff up until ten days ago when he resigned the day after Whitey Huffer was elected to take Rupert's place. I never had liked the sight of him out of uniform.

Somehow, he looked smaller and older in his jeans and plaid wool shirt.

"Is this goodbye?" I asked, returning to my chair.

He used his pocketknife to cut the top out of the Coke can. Then he spat into the can. "For the time being. Elvira and I will be leaving for El Paso, Texas, as soon as I get home. We plan to spend the winter at least."

"What's in El Paso?" I asked.

"Sunshine and lots of it. The older I get, the more I seem to need it."

Whitey Huffer sped by in his patrol car and turned south onto Ferry Street. I wondered where he was going in such a hurry.

"Besides sunshine?" I asked Rupert.

"Elvira's brother lives out there. He plans to show us the sights."

I had been to El Paso a time or two. I didn't remember all that many sights to see. "That'll take about a day," I said. "What do you plan to do then?"

Rupert studied me before spitting into the Coke can. His eyes looked even larger than usual and sadder. "You can't talk me out of it, Garth," he said. "But thanks for trying."

"You could have finished the year out at least," I said. "Given me time to get used to your being gone."

"You'll get along fine without me," he said. "And so will the town of Oakalla." He looked embarrassed. "Contrary to what you said in yesterday's paper."

"What I said about you was true."

"Maybe. But you didn't have to lay it on so thick."

I thought I saw the county coroner's car approach from the east and turn south onto Ferry Street as Whitey Huffer had done. I went to the window to see what I could see, which turned out to be nothing that I hadn't seen hundreds of times before.

"What's up?" Rupert asked, showing little interest.

I returned to my chair. "I don't know. Maybe nothing."

We sat for a while without saying anything. For the first

time in a long time, I felt uncomfortable in his presence. Perhaps because I hated goodbyes.

"It still hurts, doesn't it?" he said.

"What does?"

"Losing the election to Whitey Huffer."

"Yeah, it hurts," I said. "I don't see how so many people around here could be so stupid." But what I couldn't tell him was that losing his friendship hurt a whole lot more.

"You mean the very same people that buy your newspaper and read your column every week."

Along with publishing the *Oakalla Reporter*, I wrote a weekly syndicated column that had enjoyed modest success over the years and was still growing in circulation.

"Yeah. I guess that's what I mean," I said. "Usually the people of Oakalla listen to me. This time they didn't. It makes me wonder if I'm losing my touch."

Out of habit, he reached for the sheriff's hat he no longer wore to adjust its brim. Realizing that the hat wasn't there, he put his hand back in his lap.

"It's a lot more complicated than that, Garth," he said. "Folks around here pretty much think for themselves, whether they seem to or not. They know what Clarkie is and what he isn't. But Whitey Huffer is for the most part a mystery to them. So rather than bet on someone they take for a sure loser, they picked someone who they think might at least have a chance to do the job. It's to your credit that Clarkie did as well in the election as he did."

"I don't see how anyone can call Clarkie a loser," I said angrily. "After all he's done for this town in the past."

Again he reached for his hat. Again it wasn't there. "Think about it, Garth. With your head, not your heart, which is what you've been using through this whole thing. Would you want to be on the front line with Clarkie? Chances are, he'd get you both killed."

He had a point, but I didn't want to admit it. "I wouldn't want to be on the front line with Whitey Huffer, either. At least with Clarkie, I wouldn't always have to watch my back."

He shrugged. "Of the two of them, I don't know which one of them I'd rather trust. Neither, I guess. Though both of us know I think the world of Clarkie."

I smiled. "Are you ever going to tell him that?"

He rose and returned my smile. "Probably not."

I stood to shake his hand. But I ended up hugging him. To my surprise, he hugged me back.

"Take care of yourself," I said.

"You do the same."

"And give my love to Elvira."

"As she does to you."

That was that.

About an hour later, I saw Whitey Huffer and the county coroner return from wherever they'd been. Whitey Huffer turned west on Gas Line Road and Ben Bryan, the county coroner, turned east toward home. They were closely followed by an Operation Lifeline ambulance, which also turned east.

A few minutes later Danny Palmer drove by in his wrecker and turned south on Ferry Street. I couldn't sit still any longer. I met Chief Deputy Harold Clark on my way out my office door as he was on his way in.

"Give me a ride, Clarkie?" I said.

"Where to?"

"Wherever Danny Palmer is going in his wrecker."

"Sure, Garth. I'll be glad to."

We got into Clarkie's patrol car and caught up to the wrecker a couple blocks later when it stopped to turn southeast onto Colburn Road. From there on it was no trouble following the wrecker because Danny Palmer was in no hurry to get wherever it was he was going.

"What's up?" Clarkie said.

"I was hoping you'd tell me. Have you and Whitey been in communication at all today?"

Though he had threatened to resign, Clarkie had yet to

turn in his badge. Theoretically he had until the end of the year, but we both knew he would never last that long.

"No," he said angrily. "We haven't been in communication since the day after the election when he asked for my badge, and I wouldn't give it to him."

"So how long do you plan to hold out?"

"Not much longer, Garth. Maybe until the end of the month." He looked away so that I wouldn't see the hurt on his face. "Just long enough for me to see this town get what it deserves."

That didn't sound like the Clarkie I knew. Though Rupert was right to question Clarkie's ability under fire, and had once called Clarkie "a real-world dropout," Clarkie had a lot of savvy when it came to certain tools of his trade, computers in particular. And he took a lot of pride in his work, too. A short round balding man who would always wear his age well, Clarkie reminded me a lot of the craftsmen of old, who, if they couldn't do something right, wouldn't do it at all.

"That's only three weeks away," I said. "How much can go wrong in three weeks?"

"You might be surprised," he said. And he turned out to be right.

On Colburn Road we headed southeast in the general direction of Madison, which, as the crow flies, was about fifty miles away. As we passed the proposed site of the new Bench-Mart plaza, I saw Clarkie glance at me, then hurriedly look away. I knew what he was thinking. Here was another defeat for me, which made two within the past month.

From the beginning I had fought the Bench-Mart plaza with everything I had in the belief that once it was built, it would be the beginning of the end for Oakalla's downtown and Oakalla itself as I knew it. I had seen it happen in city after city and town after town, as they stretched out in all directions into suburbs, chain stores, mini malls, and additions. They became like every other town around, one long stretch of plazas and gas stations and fast-food restaurants that went on and on until you finally came to the town itself. Except it wasn't the same town any longer. It had lost its center and its heart, its character and its characters, and with its integrity, its identity. I didn't want the same thing to happen to Oakalla and had said so. But in the end the County Council had voted to rezone the land in question from agricultural to commercial. Now all Claire Huffer and her brother, Larry Stout, the landowners, had to do was sign on the dotted line, and it was a done deal.

"I thought Claire Huffer once told you she wouldn't sell that land for anything," Clarkie said.

"'Not for love nor money' were her exact words."

Claire Huffer had spoken them to me on my one visit to her farm when she was still Claire Stout, and I was still involved with Diana. I had done a feature on women farmers, and Claire Huffer was its star.

"I wonder what happened to change her mind," Clarkie said. "You don't suppose Whitey got to her, do you?" As he spoke, Clarkie's lip curled into a snarl. I wondered if mine did the same thing whenever I spoke about Whitey Huffer.

"I don't think so, Clarkie. As much as I don't like the man, I can't see him changing Claire's mind about that. Or anyone else changing her mind."

Claire Huffer and Larry Stout had inherited the land from their father, Warren Stout, whose estate included over two thousand acres, most of it prime farmland. Warren Stout had inherited the land from his father, who in turn had inherited it from his father, who had pioneered the land back in the 1850s. Claire Huffer had told me all of this while up to her gum boots in mud and manure. Never had I met anyone who loved her land more than she did. That included my Grandmother Ryland whose roots were sunk in the soil of Wisconsin just about as deep as roots could go.

We turned east off of Colburn Road onto Bear Hollow Road. "Something changed Claire Huffer's mind," Clarkie persisted.

"True," I said. "Something did."

Amel Pilkin's old yellow Toyota pickup was parked along Bear Hollow Road about fifty yards ahead. I had a bad feeling about the pickup as we approached it. The feeling didn't get any better when Danny Palmer parked his wrecker alongside it.

Danny got out of the wrecker. Clarkie and I got out of the patrol car. We met in the middle of Bear Hollow Road.

"What's going on?" Clarkie said to Danny. "Did Amel's old truck finally give up the ghost?"

Danny and I exchanged glances. He said that Clarkie obviously didn't know what was going on. "It's Amel who gave up the ghost, Clarkie. Orville Goodnight found him dead in his truck early this morning."

Clarkie's reaction was one of shock and dismay. I felt the same way, though I did a better job of hiding it.

"Then why didn't somebody tell me about it?" Clarkie said.

"Maybe Whitey figured he could handle it himself," Danny answered.

I walked over to Amel's pickup, which literally was held together with duct tape and baling wire. Amel had built a wooden bed for it after the old bed had rusted out, and he had filled in the rest of the rusted places with body putty that he'd never bothered to paint. But the engine itself had well over two hundred thousand miles on it and, at least up until last night, was still going strong.

"Where's all of Amel's trash?" I asked Danny, who had come over to the pickup.

"I don't know, Garth. I just got here, the same as you."

The last time I had seen Amel's pickup, it was filled with barrels of trash. Amel had a trash route throughout Adams County that he ran every day except Sunday, and every Friday evening without fail, he would stop at the Corner Bar and Grill whenever he finished his route.

I stared into the bed of the pickup, which had been swept clean of everything but a few beads of dirt. I was certain that it was full of barrels when I'd seen it last. "Do you mind if I look inside that cab?" I asked Danny. "Before you haul it away?"

"Be my guest," he said.

"Clarkie, do I have your permission?"

"Hell, Garth," he said. "Do you need to ask?"

I opened the driver's side door of the pickup and looked inside. Though it was cold enough to freeze solid the puddles alongside the road, I could still smell peach brandy inside the cab. An empty pint bottle of it lay on the seat an arm's reach away. The glove compartment was open, and Amel's worn leather work gloves lay together on the seat in front of it. Apparently he'd taken off his gloves and laid them on the seat before he opened the glove compartment and took out the bottle of brandy.

"What do you think, Garth?" Clarkie asked, while looking over my shoulder into the cab.

I nudged Clarkie out of the way and shut the door. "I don't see anything out of order," I said. "What did Ben Bryan have to say?" I asked Danny.

"He's not saying anything until after the autopsy," Danny said. "But Whitey Huffer offered the opinion that Amel's truck must have broken down, and for whatever his reasons, Amel decided to sit here and wait for help rather than walk on home. Since it was cold, he left the motor running. He fell asleep, the motor kept running, and he died from carbon-monoxide poisoning."

"There's one way to test that theory," I said, opening the driver's side door and sliding under the wheel.

But try though I might, I couldn't get the pickup to start. Neither could I get the gas gauge to register anything but empty.

"It could have happened that way," I said grudgingly after getting out of the pickup and closing the door. "But that still doesn't explain where Amel's barrels of trash went." The more I thought about it, the more certain I was that I had seen them sitting there in the bed of the pickup the previous evening.

"I don't know about that, Garth," Danny said. "You might ask Orville Goodnight."

Orville Goodnight was a retired dairy farmer who lived back a long lane off Bear Hollow Road. His was the last house before you got to Pilkin's Knob, where Amel Pilkin lived and where Bear Hollow Road ended.

Clarkie and I were about halfway up Orville Goodnight's lane when we met him in his new blue Chevy pickup on his way out of the lane. Since the lane was too narrow for us to pass, we all had to stop.

"You're blocking my lane," Orville shouted after rolling down his window and leaning part way out of it.

I got out of the patrol car to go talk to him. Clarkie stayed where he was since technically he and Orville weren't speaking to each other and hadn't for the past year. If he'd had his way, Clarkie would have pushed Orville, pickup and all, all the way back to his house.

"What of it," Clarkie shouted back. "We're here on police business."

"Says who," Orville said. "I don't see any policeman around."

Orville was a small feisty man, who loved politics almost as well as he had once loved his herd of prize Holsteins. He and Claire Huffer had headed the campaign that got Whitey Huffer elected sheriff. Orville was tired, he said, of that other party being in office all of the time.

I opened the passenger-side door and got into Orville's pickup. It was warm in there. At first the heat felt good to me.

"Who invited you in?" Orville said.

Orville had small eyes, a short pointed nose, a narrow pinched face, and a large Adam's apple that bobbed up and down whenever he spoke. He wore a red leather cap with furry red earmuffs that tied under his chin, green insulated coveralls, mittens over his gloves, and a perpetual scowl.

I smiled at him. Though Orville tried not to show it, he liked me. I was one of the few people in Oakalla who would talk politics with him. He'd either alienated or outlived most of the others.

"Okay, Garth, speak your piece," he said. "And make it snappy because I've got places to go and people to see."

"Do you mind turning down the heat a little?" I said. Already I'd started to sweat under my sheepherder's coat.

"You've got some nerve," he said, turning down the heat and turning off the fan.

"I know. But that's why you like me."

It didn't take long for Orville to tell me all that he knew about Amel Pilkin's death. He had found Amel dead in his truck when driving into town for breakfast at the Corner Bar and Grill. Amel must have been dead for some time, he said, because Amel's face felt rubbery, it was so cold.

"Did you see anybody else around the pickup or any evidence that anybody else had been there?" I asked.

"Nope. I'll tell you the same thing I told Whitey. It looked to me like Amel broke down there along Bear Hollow Road, had himself a few swallows of that peach brandy he keeps there in the truck, and fell asleep with the motor running."

"At least you and Whitey have your stories straight."

He suddenly straightened, as if someone had poked him with a cattle prod. "What's that supposed to mean?"

"Nothing. Forget I said anything."

"So are you satisfied?" Orville turned the fan back on and the heat back up.

"If you can tell me what happened to the barrels of trash that Amel had in the back of his pickup."

"What barrels of trash?" he said. "Amel's pickup was empty when I got there."

"Didn't Amel run his route yesterday?" I asked.

Orville thought a moment, then said, "Now that you mention it, I'm almost sure he did. Though he neglected to stop by my place." Orville's face was forgiving. "Which, of course, is understandable if he was dead."

"Are you his last stop on Friday?"

"His last or his first, depending on his mood."

"Do you know the others on his Friday route?"

"A few of them. But Amel has all of them written down in that route book of his. If you can read his chicken tracks. I never could."

I opened the door and stepped out into an icy cold west wind. "Thanks, Orville. You've been a big help."

"Now all you've got to do is get pea-brain there to move his patrol car," he said grimly. "What are the odds of that?"

The odds of that would have been better if, the moment I got inside the patrol car, Orville hadn't pulled forward, then begun to race his engine and blow his horn.

"If that little weasel thinks I'm going to back out of here," Clarkie said through clenched teeth, "he's got another think coming."

"Do whatever you like," I said. "We've got all winter to sit here."

"Would you back out, if you were me?"

"That depends, Clarkie, on what I planned on doing for the rest of my life. As old as he is, Orville's bound to die before we do."

"You think I'm being stubborn, don't you?"

"No, Clarkie, I think you're being stupid. But not any stupider than I am because I'm right here with you."

In the end Clarkie backed out of the lane. He still didn't want to, but he knew Orville Goodnight as well as I did, and once Orville took a position on something, he never backed down from it. I had once said that it would take an act of Congress to change Orville's mind. Ruth had answered that it would take an act of God.

3

PILKIN'S KNOB, WHICH was named for the three generations of Pilkins who had lived there, sat atop a limestone outcropping, overlooking the east fork of Stony Creek. The original house had fallen in about ten years ago, and Amel Pilkin had used the remaining good boards from it to build a smaller house on the same foundation. The result was not a spectacular success, since the house leaned to one side and had only one window in it, but from the outside at least, it looked weathertight, and liveable, if you were either a Stoic or groundhog.

I got out of the patrol car and stood a moment in the clearing there beside Amel's house. Below me I could see the rutted remains of the old roadbed and below that the dark swift waters of Stony Creek. Bear Hollow Road hadn't always ended at Pilkin's Knob. But in June 1957, or so Ruth told me, a series of heavy rains one on top of the other, followed by a goose drowner, had washed out the bridge below Pilkin's Knob and left it high and dry. From that time on, like Navoe Cemetery northwest of Oakalla where the road also ended, Pilkin's Knob was a dead end.

I opened the only door to the house and went inside with Clarkie right at my heels. The house was dim, musty, and cool. Already it felt abandoned.

"Aren't there any lights in here?" Clarkie said.

"Not that I can find."

Then I discovered the kerosene lantern that hung on a nail to the left of the door. A box of blue-tip kitchen matches sat on a four-by-four just above the lantern. I lit the lantern, adjusted its wick, then went on inside.

A wood stove that fed into a red brick chimney sat at the north end of the room. Amel's box spring and mattress sat on the floor at the south end. A green wood table and two paint-splattered green wood chairs stood in the middle of the room. Along the east wall was the house's only window. Beneath the window were a pitcher pump and sink and beside the sink was an old-fashioned ice chest with ice, milk, bread, and bologna in it. A little further along the east wall was a toilet with no lid or handle and a five-gallon bucket of water sitting on the floor beside it. Along the west wall was a fuzzy green couch. A kerosene lamp stood on a small table at one end of the couch and a stack of old magazines and old newspapers slouched against the other end of it. I guessed that Amel read the magazines and used the newspapers to light his stove.

I felt the stove. It was barely warm. But when I dug with a poker deep into its ashes, I uncovered some live coals. Amel had a fire in there recently, probably as recently as yesterday morning.

"I'm going outside," Clarkie said, rubbing his hands on his pants.

"I'll be with you in a minute."

Holding the lantern out in front of me as I took one more tour of the room, I was reminded of Frost's words, "like an old-stone savage armed." The lantern was my weapon. I used it to keep the dark at bay.

Finding nothing out of place, I blew out the lantern, hung it where I'd found it, and went outside. Cold though it was, it felt good to be outside again.

"What a way to live," Clarkie said.

I blew on my hands to warm them. "People used to live that way all of the time."

"Yeah," he said. "And we call them the good old days."

"In some ways they were."

"In some ways they weren't, too."

We walked around back. To our left was a lean-to with a tin roof where Amel kept his firewood, chain saw, axe, splitting maul, and the kerosene for his lamps. Directly ahead was the shed where he stored and separated his trash. What he could recycle, he took to Madison every other Sunday afternoon. What he couldn't recycle went into the ravine behind the shed.

Several unsorted barrels of trash sat on the dirt floor inside the storage shed, and, even in the cold, they stank. Clarkie took one whiff and nearly ran over me in his haste to get out of there. Clarkie had a notoriously weak stomach. In Ruth's eyes, it was one of the things that had cost him the election, since, in her words, "people couldn't take a green-in-the-gills sheriff seriously." After dumping a couple of the barrels and seeing what was inside, I wished I had followed Clarkie's lead.

"Find anything?" Clarkie asked as I stepped outside.

"No. I can't tell by looking at them whether these are the same barrels I saw in Amel's truck last night or not."

"Are you sure you saw any barrels in Amel's truck last night?" Clarkie said.

"Sure enough," I said, showing him my shoes, "to dump somebody's spaghetti dinner all over me."

We then walked to the edge of the ravine where Amel dumped the trash he couldn't recycle, and while Clarkie stood there watching me, I waded in. But after searching through the mass of cans, bottles, barrels, and appliances that had grown chest-deep over the years, I found nothing that had been worth going down there for. So we left.

"What were you hoping to find?" Clarkie asked me on our way back to Oakalla.

"Some evidence that Amel made it home last night."

"Why is that important?"

"Think about it, Clarkie. If he never made it home, where

did all of the barrels of trash go that I believe were in the back of his pickup? If he had made it home, which it doesn't look like he did, but it's still a possibility, then why did he go out again? In either case, I have to wonder."

"Oh," was all he said.

4

CLARKIE LET ME off at the *Oakalla Reporter* where I spent the rest of the morning sitting at my desk, staring at the wall. I couldn't shake the memory of those last few dying coals in Amel's stove. Once they burned out and the stove went completely cold, Amel's last link with this life would be severed. He might live on in someone's memory, or in another place, or in another form, but Amel, as I knew him, would be gone.

I called the county coroner, Ben Bryan, at his home. "Ben, this is Garth Ryland. I understand you have Amel Pilkin there."

"For the time being," he said. "But on Monday he goes to Madison."

"For burial?" I couldn't see Amel being buried anywhere except Oakalla.

"For research. He willed his body to the medical school there at the University of Wisconsin."

"You've seen the will?"

"Nope. There was never anything written down, just an understanding that Amel and I had. The way he expressed it to me, he hoped they'd get more good out of his body than Amel Pilkin ever did. Those were his exact words, or at least what I took them to be. 'Than Amel Pilkin ever did.' Anyway," he continued, "I've notified the people there, and as soon as we're done with him here, they're coming after him."

I glanced out my north window and thought I saw a couple flakes of snow. "So his death was an accident?"

He hesitated before answering. I watched for more snow but didn't see any. "He died of carbon-monoxide poisoning. So from all appearances, his death was an accident."

"From all appearances?"

He sighed, as if sorry now that he'd said anything. "It's nothing to hang your hat on, Garth, even though I know how your mind runs. There's a contusion on the back of Amel's head that I can't explain. That's all."

"And?" I believed there had to be more, or he wouldn't have told me that much.

"And even though Amel's clothes smelled like he'd been swimming in peach brandy, I didn't find much alcohol in his blood. Just a trace really. Not enough to warrant him smelling like he did."

"Which means what?" A burst of snow blew by my window, like smoke from a gun.

"Which means it's not all nice, neat, and tidy the way I'd like it to be."

"Have you told Whitey Huffer what you found?"

"I told him. But he didn't take the news well. He's all for calling it an accident and getting on with things."

"Which you're not willing to do?"

"I didn't say that, Garth. From all appearances, it was an accident. Unless you know something I don't."

What did I know that might make Ben Bryan look a little closer at Amel's death? Nothing for certain. Nothing I could print with a clear conscience, which was my test for certainty.

"I know, in my own mind anyway, that when Amel left Oakalla last night, he was carrying a load of trash in the bed of his pickup. And when I saw his pickup this morning, it was empty."

He thought about my words, then said, "Are you sure about the trash?"

It was my turn to think. Had I really seen the barrels of

trash in the back of Amel's pickup, or had I assumed they were there because they were always there before? "I don't know, Ben. I honestly can't say for certain. But his truck's been full of trash every other Friday night that it's been sitting there."

"We're not talking about every other Friday night. We're talking about last night."

"Let me ask around and see what other people say. In the meantime, do you mind if I get a second opinion?"

"About what?"

"About Amel Pilkin and how he died."

"What is it, Garth," he said, sounding hurt, "don't you trust me?"

"Trust has nothing to do with it, Ben. I just want a second opinion. You said yourself you had some doubts."

"Come ahead then," he said. "But I have to be gone this afternoon. So you and Doc will have to let yourselves in."

I smiled at his perception. "How did you know it was Doc that I'd be bringing along?"

"Who else, Garth? Who else?"

I stopped at the Marathon service station on my way to the Corner Bar and Grill for lunch. The wind was in my face the whole time, and occasionally a snowflake would burn my cheek. But even though the darkening sky promised snow, I knew it wouldn't snow. Not with a west wind and a rising barometer.

I went inside the Marathon, where Danny Palmer was putting snow tires on Cleon Metzger's old red-and-white Oldsmobile Ninety-eight. Sniffy Smith, my barber, who only cut hair on Fridays now that he was retired, sat on his favorite loafing stool, keeping Danny company. I pulled up a stool and sat down beside Sniffy.

"What's up, Garth?" Sniffy said. Before I could answer, he went on. "I suppose you heard that Amel Pilkin died."

Small and plump with sad eyes and a ready smile, Sniffy had earned his nickname because he had the habit of sniffing loudly whenever he got excited. He spent most of his days at the Marathon, helping Danny watch the drive and man the wrecker. Most of his nights he spent in the same place—either there or at the Corner Bar and Grill where I sometimes kept him company.

"I heard about Amel," I said to Sniffy.

"The sad part of it is," Sniffy said, "I hear there's not even going to be a funeral. They're going to ship his body off to Madison for a bunch of college kids to cut on."

"Who told you that?"

"Whitey Huffer." Then he straightened and sniffed in indignation. "*Sheriff* Huffer. Excuse me all to hell."

"Did Whitey set you straight on that?" I asked.

"Did he ever," Danny said with a smile.

Using an air wrench, Danny quickly loosened the lug nuts and took the left rear tire off of the Oldsmobile Ninety-eight. Just as quickly, he put the snow tire in its place and tightened the lug nuts again. He did it so easily that it didn't look like work to me. But that was the sign of a true craftsman. He could make hard work look easy.

"You have a chance to look over Amel's pickup?" I said to Danny before he could move around to the other side of the car.

"Not much of one. Why do you ask?" He checked the pressure in the snow tire he'd just put on and added some more air.

"I just wondered if there was anything wrong with the pickup that would have caused Amel to stop where he did."

Danny rose, went to the back of the Marathon, and returned with a universal joint. "This fell off of Amel's pickup the minute I hooked onto it," he said. "It looks to me like the U-joint let loose, and he had just enough power to get off the road."

"Which is why they found him dead this morning," I said.

Danny took the universal joint back to where he'd found it, then moved his air hose and wrench around to the other side of the Oldsmobile. "That appears to be the case."

I slid from the stool onto the concrete floor of the

Marathon. My feet were so cold they hurt when I landed. "Thanks, Danny. That's what I wanted to know."

"You don't have to rush off," Sniffy said, wanting my company.

"I'm on my way to lunch," I said. "Otherwise, I'd stay longer."

" A man has to eat," Sniffy agreed.

"This man anyway." Then I stopped at the door to ask, "Sniffy, did you by any chance see Amel's pickup when it was parked in front of the hardware last evening?"

"I saw it parked there. Why?"

"Did you happen to see into the bed? What I mean is, was it full or empty?"

Sniffy scratched his chin as he thought about it. "Full, I guess. But I don't rightly know."

"How about you, Danny? Do you remember seeing it?" I asked.

"I remember seeing it," he said. "But not there. I remember meeting Amel on Colburn Road when I had to make a wrecker run south of town."

"Was it empty or full?"

Danny shook his head. "To be honest, Garth, I never paid that much attention."

I thanked them for their help and left.

As it usually was at noon on Saturday, the Corner Bar and Grill was filled, and if you wanted a seat, you had to share a table with someone else or sit on a stool at the counter. I almost always sat at the counter. And almost always on the same stool.

Bernice Phillips, the owner and noon waitress, came to take my order. I couldn't decide between beef-and-noodles and ham-and-beans, so I ordered a cheeseburger with fried onions and a piece of pumpkin pie. Normally I drank a glass of milk with lunch, but instead I ordered coffee in the hope that it would warm me up.

Whitey Huffer came in the west door of the lunchroom and walked on through to the barroom where he took a seat at the bar. It suddenly grew quiet in the lunchroom, as all of the loud, good-natured exchanges going on around me changed to whispers. I wondered why until I saw that Whitey Huffer was in uniform. In his twelve years on the job, Rupert Roberts had never sat at the bar while in uniform.

Bernice brought me my lunch. I ate slowly, as was my custom, savoring every bite. Soon I'd have to go out into the cold again. I wanted lunch to last as long as possible.

Bernice refilled my coffee cup. I sat for several seconds watching the steam rise from it before I reached for the sugar. So Amel Pilkin was dead. What did that have to do with me?

A few minutes later I stood at the cash register, waiting to pay for my lunch. I glanced into the barroom but didn't see Whitey Huffer anywhere.

"Bernice," I said when she came to take my money. "Did you see Whitey Huffer leave?"

She leaned over the counter and looked into the barroom. "No. Isn't he still in there?" she said.

"Nowhere I can see."

"Then he must have left."

I paid Bernice and left a dollar on the counter on my way into the barroom. Like Amel Pilkin the night before, Whitey had left his beer half drunk on the bar.

"Did you see where Whitey Huffer went?" I asked Hiram.

He looked around the barroom and seemed surprised to find Whitey gone. "No. I can't say I did," he said.

"Did he say anything to you before he left?"

"He was asking about Amel Pilkin, if he'd by chance left anything here on the bar last night. I told him he'd left his route book and about twenty dollars in change, which I'd left with Bernice to give to Amel if he came in this morning. 'Nothing else?' Whitey said. I said no. He sat there for a couple of minutes longer. Then, the next thing I know, he's gone."

"His patrol car's still parked outside."

Hiram looked out the window. "So it is."

I went down the basement stairs as if on my way to the restroom, but once I saw the men's restroom was empty, I continued on past the wine cellar to the basement that led under Sniffy Smith's barber shop. I had forgotten how dark it was under there. And how many cobwebs there were. I had to stop every few feet to find my way and to wipe the cobwebs from my face. But I never could get them all.

I came to the brick wall that separated the basement of the barber shop from the basement of the hardware. Feeling my way along it, I searched for the hole I knew was there. The hole was level with the ground and just wide enough for me to get my shoulders through without pinching them.

I had all of me through it but my feet when I heard a movement to my left. Instinctively, I rolled to the right and heard something thud into the soft dirt where my head had been an instant before. But when I tried to scramble forward and get to my feet at the same time, my right shoe hooked the wall and tripped me. Then something hit me squarely across my shoulders and flattened me. Stunned, I lay there waiting for a second blow to smash into my head. It never came.

I lay there longer than I needed to. Part of me wanted to move. Part of me was afraid to try to move, only to find out that I couldn't. I sat up. Then wiggled my fingers and my toes. But when I tried to stand, I felt so wobbly that I had to sit back down and wait a few minutes before trying again.

The second time that I stood, I managed to reach the steps that led up into the hardware before I had to sit down. On the third try I made it all the way up the steps, through the hardware, and out its front door.

5

WHITEY HUFFER'S PATROL car was no longer parked outside the Corner Bar and Grill. Neither did I see it parked in front of the jewelry store, post office, bank, Five and Dime, or anywhere else along Jackson Street. Nor did Whitey Huffer drive by in it while I stood there. Good thing for him, he didn't. I probably would have flipped him the bird.

I went in the side door of the Corner Bar and Grill, through the barroom, and back out to the cash register. "Weren't you just here a few minutes ago?" Bernice Phillips asked.

"I can't seem to stay away," I said. Her few minutes seemed like hours to me. "What I was wondering was, do you still have that route book that Hiram left for you to give to Amel Pilkin?"

"It's right here under the counter. Why?"

"I'd like to borrow it for a couple days. I'll bring it back to you first thing Monday morning."

She reached under the counter and handed the route book to me. "You can keep it if you like. I've got no use for it."

"Thanks, Bernice. I might just do that."

I walked home. Ruth was vacuuming the hallway upstairs, so I had to step around her on my way to the bathroom. I took off my coat, shirt, and T-shirt and stood with my back to the mirror to see if I could see where I'd been hit.

Ruth came to the door and knocked. "Need any help?" she asked.

I wondered how she knew. "It's open," I said. "How bad is it?" I asked, after she'd opened the door.

She came on into the bathroom for a closer look. "There's a red welt across your shoulders," she said, touching it just hard enough to make me wince. "But that's all I can see."

"That's all?" I said. "For a while there I thought my back was broken."

"What happened to you anyway?" She moved back out of the way so that I could get dressed again.

"Whitey Huffer hit me with his nightstick. Or whatever they call them these days. Rupert never carried one."

"Those days are gone, Garth. You might as well get used to it."

"Fat chance," I said.

We went downstairs where Amel Pilkin's route book lay on the kitchen table. "What's this?" Ruth said, picking up the route book and thumbing through it.

"It's Amel Pilkin's route book."

"I know that. What are you doing with it?"

So then I told her about what had happened to Amel Pilkin and why I happened to be in the basement of the hardware at the same time as Whitey Huffer. When I finished, she looked upset. I knew she liked Amel, but I didn't think she'd take his death so personally. Knowing Ruth, I should have known better.

"I must be slipping," she said.

Then I realized why she was so upset. Half of Oakalla knew about Amel Pilkin before she did. "So much for Amel," I said.

She gave me a look that singed my eyebrows. "And I don't need your sarcasm either."

"Sorry, Ruth. It's been that kind of day."

"Unless you change your attitude, it's probably not going to get a whole lot better."

"I'll work on it," I said on my way out the back door.

Parked in my garage was Jezebel, alias Jessie, Grandmother Ryland's brown Chevy sedan that she had willed to
me along with her eighty-acre farm and the money to buy
the *Oakalla Reporter*. Jessie had never run right for grandmother. In all of the years that I'd owned her, she'd never
run right for me, either. Ruth hated Jessie and, except in an
emergency, refused to ride in her. I both loved and hated her.
I loved her for the way she felt, solid and comfortable, and
the way she smelled, which was exactly like the dusty
machinery shed where grandmother always parked her. I
hated her for her fickleness, her incontinence, and her
insubordination under fire.

William T. Airhart, or Doc, as we in Oakalla all called
him, was the closest thing that we had to a celebrity. In the
1930s he had moved to Oakalla from Cleveland where he
had been Cuyahoga County coroner and had begun a private
practice that had lasted fifty years until he retired. During
the most of those years he had served as Adams County
coroner and as a surgeon at the county hospital.

The way I'd always heard it was that while in Cleveland,
Doc had been ranked among the top ten surgeons in the
world. Doc neither confirmed nor denied that ranking. He
said that whatever he was, it was too long ago to count one
way or another.

Doc lived across the street from the United Methodist
Church in a big white frame house with stone pillars. I drove
there, climbed the steps, knocked on his front door, and then
waited for him to answer it. For the past few years, Doc had
been writing his memoirs, so he didn't welcome interrup-
tions.

"Who is it?" he finally asked from inside.

"Garth Ryland."

"I'm not home. Come back tomorrow."

"It can't wait that long."

He opened the door to let me in. "Of course it can wait,"
he said. "You just think it can't."

A small spritely man with white hair and merry blue eyes,

Doc walked with a slight limp from having one leg shorter than the other. His walk had slowed some in the years that I had known him, but his mind was as keen as it ever was.

I followed him into his living room where he had a fire going in the fireplace and where Belle's favorite rug still lay on the hardwood floor in front of the hearth. For ten years in a row, Doc and I had grouse hunted together at least once every fall and had never shot that first grouse. This year, which would have been our eleventh, Doc's ancient setter, Belle, had died two days before the start of grouse season, and neither one of us had the heart to go without her. So on the opening day of grouse season, we sat in front of Doc's fireplace, drank J & B scotch straight up, and shared our favorite memories of her.

Doc had been typing his memoirs at a card table in front of the fire. I walked over to the card table and glanced at what he'd written that day. "When are you going to let me read this?"

"Probably never," he said.

"There are a lot of people around Oakalla who feel the same way I do. They can't wait to read them."

"Well, they're just going to have to wait," he said. "Particularly if you keep interrupting me every whipstitch."

He sat down in his easy chair. I sat down on the couch. "I guess you haven't heard that they found Amel Pilkin dead along Bear Hollow Road this morning," I said.

He sighed, glancing from me to the fireplace. "No. I hadn't heard." His eyes turned to me. I could see the fire still in them. "Why is it when you come, you always bring me good news?"

"Habit, I guess. Did you know Amel?"

"I delivered him. Breech birth and all, out there on Pilkin's Knob. It's a wonder that he or his mother, either one, survived."

"Part of your memoirs?"

"No. But it should be."

A few minutes later, we drove to Ben Bryan's house,

which sat just east of Park Street at the east end of Oakalla. The house was large, white, and nearly square. Two of the largest silver maples left in Oakalla grew along its west side. To the east were a yard, a garden, and then farm fields, all November brown and bare.

We went down the outside steps into the basement where Amel Pilkin lay naked on top of a stainless steel table in what used to be the coal bin. He looked even smaller in death than he had been in life, and cold, lying there on top of that steel table with nothing on. I fought the urge to take off my coat and cover him up.

"Would you rather wait outside?" Doc asked.

"How long are you going to be?"

"That depends on what I find."

"I'd rather wait outside."

Since the park was only a block away, I went there, took a tour of the shelter house, went to the baseball diamond where I used a stick and dirt clod to hit a clean single to left and ran to first base for old time's sake, and started back. On the way I noticed that the western sky had cleared and that a solid band of white sunlight separated the blue from the grey where the clouds met the sky. God was in His heaven. All should be right with the world.

Doc came out of the basement just as I started down the basement steps. "Ready?" I said.

"Ready."

"So what's the verdict?" I asked, once we were inside Jessie and on our way again.

"No verdict," he said. "I found nothing there to dispute Ben's findings. He could've hit his head on something, or somebody could've hit him over the head. He's got a knot there, that's for sure, and he got it just a short while before he died. But how short of a while, I don't know. What I mean is, I can't pin it down to hours and minutes."

"I suppose he could've hit his head while making good his escape," I said.

"His escape from what?"

"The Corner Bar and Grill. He took off through the basement to the hardware while Ruth and I were sitting in there."

"Who was he running from?" Doc asked.

I came to the stop sign and turned west on Gas Line Road. "I don't know. Whitey Huffer came into the bar right about the time that Amel took off, but that could've been a coincidence. Except Whitey came back again a few minutes later and stayed only long enough to see that Amel wasn't there. Then today at noon Whitey retraced Amel's journey under the hardware." I straightened my shoulders. They still were sore where he'd hit me. "At least I think it was Whitey who was under there with me."

We passed the white concrete-block building that housed the *Oakalla Reporter* and continued west on Gas Line Road.

"Why would Whitey Huffer be looking for Amel?" Doc asked.

"I don't know." I turned to look at Doc, who probably knew more about the people of Oakalla than anyone else except for Ruth and her Aunt Emma. "You wouldn't happen to know, would you?"

"No, Garth, I wouldn't. Since I gave up my practice, I don't get around as much as I used to."

"So there's nothing you can tell me about either Amel Pilkin or Whitey Huffer that you think I should know?"

"I can tell you that Whitey Huffer's no Rupert Roberts," he said. "And that it might be wise if you didn't cross him."

I turned left on Perrin Street and then left into Doc's driveway four houses later. "It's too late for that, Doc. I've already crossed him."

"Then watch your tail." He got out of Jessie and limped up the steps to his house.

I drove home and parked Jessie in the garage. Just as I came in the back door, somebody knocked on the front door. I didn't like his knock. It was loud and insistent, like that of someone who thought he belonged inside whether you wanted him there or not.

"I'm coming," I yelled, wondering where Ruth was. "Hold your horses."

Whitey Huffer stood at the front door. He seemed no more pleased to see me than I was to see him. Perhaps even less so.

"All right, Ryland, where is it?" he said, pushing open the door and stepping inside before I even got there.

"Where is what?"

He'd left the door wide open. As I stepped toward him to close it, his hand went to his gun. "Hold it right there."

"Then shut the door yourself," I said, stopping short of him.

He took his hand off his gun. I stepped around him and closed the door.

"You know what I'm after," he said. "Amel Pilkin's route book. I want it. And I want it now."

"Why?"

"What do you mean *why*?" he said. Already flush from the cold, his face grew even redder. "I don't have to tell you why. I'm the sheriff, not you."

Whitey wore a slick brown leather jacket over his blue uniform, white calfskin gloves that matched his hair, but no hat, despite the cold. As I thought about it, I had never seen Whitey Huffer wear a hat. Maybe I could get him one for Christmas.

"Unless you're conducting an official investigation into Amel Pilkin's death, you have to tell me why," I said. "Otherwise, I have as much right to that route book as you do."

Whitey's face darkened even more, and the veins popped out on his forehead. Then he took a deep breath and slowly let it out. I could smell booze on his breath. I hated to smell booze on the breath of anyone carrying a gun. Particularly if the carrier didn't like me.

"Do I have to get mean?" he said.

"No. All you have to do is tell me why you want Amel's route book. It's that simple."

He reached for his nightstick. But he never got the chance to use it because at that moment Ruth came out of the downstairs bathroom carrying the route book.

"Here," she said, handing him the book. "Is this what you wanted?"

He took it from her, turned to leave, then turned back to me again with his legs spread for balance and his hand on his nightstick. "Just for the hell of it," he said, "I ought to work you over anyway."

I didn't wait to see if he meant it. I kicked him in the groin, then before he could recover, shoved him out the door and down the steps to the sidewalk.

"That wasn't a smart thing to do," Ruth said on my return.

I reached inside the front closet where I kept my single-shot sixteen gauge Stevens, broke open the Stevens, and put a shell into it. "Probably not," I said. "But it felt good."

I kept my eye on Whitey Huffer who finally got to his feet, took a long look at the house, and got into his patrol car and drove away. I sighed a huge sigh of relief because at any moment I had expected him to draw his gun and charge back up the stairs. Then I ejected the shell from the Stevens and put the Stevens away.

"A lot of help you were," I said to Ruth. "Why didn't you just hand over the rest of the house while you were at it."

Without a word, she went into the bathroom and returned a moment later with what looked to be a couple of pages from Amel Pilkin's route book. She handed them to me.

"What are these?" I said.

"You have all of the answers," she snapped. "You figure them out."

I looked at the pages that Ruth had given me, but I was too charged up to try to make any sense out of them. Rarely did I act in haste and almost never with violence. I wondered what had happened to me.

"Maybe another time," I said, tossing them onto the couch.

"They're the whole of Amel's Friday route," she said. "Every single stop is on them."

I stared at the pages for several seconds. I felt humble, grateful, and foolish. "I wish you'd said something sooner," I said.

She glared at me the way only Ruth could glare. She might forgive me by April, but then that was probably expecting too much. "And when did I have the time?" she said.

"Well, it's too late now to take it back," I said. "Either from you or Whitey Huffer."

"I wouldn't worry about me, Garth. I'll get over it. I'm not so sure about Whitey Huffer."

"The sonofabitch had no right to threaten me in my own house," I said, still angry. "Some things are sacred. My house is one of them."

"And Whitey Huffer himself had nothing to do with it?" she asked.

I shrugged. "Maybe a little."

"Maybe a lot."

I went to the front door to look outside where the sun was just about to set in a flawless blue sky. Maybe a lot, she had said. As always, she was right.

6

IT WAS DARK. Ruth and the rest of her bowling team members were on their way to Wisconsin Rapids to bowl a practice match in preparation for their Thanksgiving tournament, which was coming up in a couple weeks. I was on my way to the Corner Bar and Grill to kill another Saturday night.

Ruth and I had both glanced through the pages she had taken from Amel Pilkin's route book, but except for the names of Amel's Friday customers, found nothing there of interest. Whatever Whitey Huffer's reasons were for wanting the route book, we didn't learn them.

"What'll it be, Garth?" Hiram asked as I sat down at the bar.

I looked around the barroom and counted five others besides Hiram and me. A few more might be in the back room playing euchre, and some might have come in early for supper and then left early. But all things considered, it was a slow Saturday night at the Corner Bar and Grill.

"Nothing right now, thanks," I said. "Actually, I came in to talk to you."

Hiram smiled at that. A lot of people came into the Corner Bar and Grill to talk to him, whether they knew it or not.

"Fire away," he said.

"You remember when Amel Pilkin was in here last night?" I said. "How he kept jabbering away at me? For the life of me, I can't figure out what he was trying so hard to say. I just wondered if you had any thoughts on the matter."

"Nary a one," he said with regret. "Usually I could get the gist of what he was trying to say, even if I didn't understand every word. But last night it was like he was speaking another language altogether."

"Then I'm not the only one who thinks so," I said. I found some comfort in that.

"No, Garth. You're not the only one who thinks so."

Hiram made his rounds while I waited for him to return. It was too quiet in there for me to think. I wished somebody would play the jukebox.

"You're sure I can't get you something?" Hiram said on his return. "It's on the house."

"A cup of Irish coffee then," I said, not wanting to offend the house. "But make it a light one."

When he brought it to me a couple minutes later, I took a sip and smiled my approval. Hiram had used real whipped cream in his Irish coffee, and real Irish whiskey. I could feel it warm me all the way down to my toes.

"Thanks," I said. "It hits the spot."

"I thought it might."

"I have another question, Hiram," I said, "while we're on the subject. Have you ever seen Amel as excited as he was last night? I mean so excited that he couldn't even make himself understood."

"Only once that I recall," he said, moving down the bar to wipe up some spilled beer. "A bunch of the young studs around town had fixed Amel up with Debbie Patrick, the town whore. Amel thought for sure he was going to get laid that night. He got so excited he couldn't keep either his mouth closed or his hands off his zipper."

"Did he get laid?"

"No. Debbie stood him up. She came into the bar, took one look at him, and left. She said loud enough for everyone in the place but Amel to hear that she wasn't going to screw, in her words, 'no retarded dwarf.'"

"How did Amel take it?" I asked.

Hiram smiled. I could see sadness in it. "About like he took everything else. You knew Amel. Nothing kept him down for very long."

I thought about all the times I'd seen Amel Pilkin around Oakalla. Even when he was down on his luck, he never looked defeated. Weary perhaps. That couldn't be helped. And almost always out of place. But never defeated. He had too much pride for that. And too great a spirit.

"I was out to Pilkin's Knob today," I said. "Did you know that he didn't have any electricity there?"

"I'd heard that," Hiram said. "But he's not the only one around who lives like that. Beat the bushes someday, Garth. You'd be surprised at what you might find."

"That sounds like something I ought to write about," I said.

"It wouldn't hurt," he said. "Especially with winter coming on."

I finished my Irish coffee a few minutes later. A few minutes after that I slid from the barstool and hoped my feet hit the floor. I'd told Hiram to make it a light one. Maybe he thought I meant the whipped cream.

"Hiram, I'm going down to the basement," I said. "If I don't come back right away, don't worry about it."

"Is there something down there I should know about?" he said. "First there was Amel last evening, then you and Whitey Huffer today noon. Now you're going back down there again."

"Trouble, Hiram," I said, testing my legs to see if I could walk a straight line. "The only thing down there is trouble."

"Might be good place to stay away from then."

If only I could, Hiram. If only I could.

I'd brought a pocket flashlight from home, and I used it sparingly to search the restrooms and the wine cellar and then to find my way from the basement of the Corner Bar and Grill to the basement of the hardware. But even with the light, I couldn't miss all of the cobwebs or escape the uneasy feeling that basements seemed to breed in me. In some ways I liked basements better in the dark. Then I couldn't see their walls closing in on me.

Heard the floor of the hardware creak. Someone with hard heels was on the floor above me, walking my way. I turned off my flashlight, stood very still, and waited to see what would happen. Then I heard voices, men's voices by the sound of them. One of the voices belonged to Whitey Huffer.

"I tell you it's got to be here someplace," Whitey said. "If he'd had it with him, I would've found it in his truck."

The other man said something I couldn't understand.

"I know there'll be hell to pay when Claire finds out," Whitey said. "Don't you think I know that."

Whitey's companion said something else. It sounded like a warning.

"Who's going to hear us?" Whitey said. "And what can they do about it if they do? I'm the sheriff, remember."

I didn't hear the other man clearly, but it sounded as if he said, "Who could forget."

They moved to another part of the store, and even though I tried to follow along beneath them, I didn't hear them say anything else. Then they left. So either they had found what they were looking for or grown tired of looking. I hoped it was the latter.

I retraced my steps back to the Corner Bar and Grill. I could always search the hardware in the daylight when Whitey Huffer couldn't arrest me for breaking and entering.

"Find anything?" Hiram asked when I emerged from the basement.

"No," I said, brushing the cobwebs from my hair. "You haven't by any chance seen Whitey Huffer in here, have you?"

"No. Not that I recall."

"How about earlier this evening?"

"Not then either."

Determined to find out who Whitey Huffer's companion had been, I left the barroom by the side door and emerged along Jackson Street. But I didn't see Whitey Huffer anywhere. I went around to the front of the Corner Bar and Grill and looked up and down Glick Street, but I didn't see him there either. Or any sign of his patrol car, which, I guessed, had been parked in back of the hardware when he was in there. Apparently Whitey Huffer had left, taking his companion with him. Not knowing what else to do, I went home.

7

THE NEXT MORNING I was awakened by the smell of coffee perking. I went downstairs where Ruth sat at the kitchen table in her ratty pink housecoat that had come over on the Mayflower and in the fur-lined moccasins that I'd bought for her at the Big Charlie's four Christmases ago. My shoulders ached where Whitey Huffer had hit me with his nightstick. My nose felt as if I had been snuffing barbed wire. And my head hurt for reasons of its own. But other than that, I felt fine.

"How cold is it anyway?" I asked Ruth.

I'd heard the furnace run most of the night. I always listened for the furnace, particularly when fuel oil was the price it was, to tell me when it was really cold outside.

"Ten above when I looked," she said.

"It's a good thing there isn't any snow on the ground, or it would be ten below."

I poured myself a cup of coffee, added half-and-half and a teaspoon and a half of sugar, and sat down at the table across from Ruth. For a long time, even when I still went to church regularly—or perhaps because I still went to church regularly—Sunday depressed me. After my son died, now twelve years ago, I could barely face each Sunday morning. Lately, however, I had learned to like Sunday a little better. Not as well as Friday or Saturday, but at least as well as Tuesday.

"Well, how did things go last night?" I asked Ruth.

"They went," she said sourly. "But at least Liddy Bennett's ball ended up in the same lane that it started in every time. And Wanda Collum marked in three of her frames."

"That's progress."

"Not much."

Ruth took her bowling seriously. One bad night and she was talking to her ball. Two bad nights and she was sleeping with it.

"So how did your night go?" she said.

"Not bad. If you like cobwebs up your nose."

"After what happened last time, I thought you weren't going back under there again."

"I wasn't. But I changed my mind." I took a sip of coffee and felt better. "Whitey Huffer and a male companion were in the hardware after hours last night. You have any idea who that companion might be?"

She sat hoarding her last swallow of coffee, like a miser his last dollar. Once that was gone, she would have to get up and fix breakfast.

"I heard Whitey's brother-in-law, Larry Stout, rode patrol with him last weekend. That might be who it was."

"It stands to reason," I said. "Because whoever he was, he mentioned Claire Huffer."

Ruth's antennae went up. She had a knack of learning all of my weaknesses. "What did he have to say about Claire Huffer?"

"Only that there would be hell to pay when she found out."

"Found out what?"

"I don't know. That's what the mystery is. I don't know what Whitey Huffer is looking for, or why he's looking for it."

She drank the last of her coffee, then rose and walked to the stove where she took out her favorite black iron skillet and set it on the right front burner. "Are you sure he's looking for something, Garth? Besides any excuse to shoot you."

"He's not going to shoot me."

"Don't be too sure of that." She took a package of fresh sausage from the refrigerator and began to make patties.

"And to answer your question," I said, "yes, I'm sure he's looking for something. And I'm equally sure that Amel Pilkin has, or had, whatever Whitey's looking for."

"How can Amel still have it if he's dead?" she asked.

"Maybe it's somewhere on Pilkin's Knob. Maybe he left it there before he came to town. Or left it there on his way home from town, though that's looking more and more unlikely."

She put the sausage patties in the skillet, wiped her hands with a paper towel, and lit the burner. "What could Amel Pilkin possibly have that anybody would want? He was as poor as a church mouse, Garth. And he wouldn't know something of value if he was looking right at it."

"That's just my point, Ruth. Maybe somebody threw it away Friday by mistake. And now Whitey Huffer is trying to get it back again."

She washed her hands in the sink, wiped them, then picked up the pages she'd torn from Amel's route book. "Well, let's just see about that. Who on these pages is likely to have thrown away the store by mistake? Ned Ruarch? Not a likely candidate there. Roosevelt was president the last time he threw anything away."

"Teddy or FDR?"

She glared at me and went on. "Frank and Jo Ellen Henderson? Not likely candidates, either. They've never owned anything worth keeping. The Apple brothers? There's a possibility there since they're both getting up in years. But they wouldn't remember it if they did throw it away."

She read on through the pages, enjoying herself at my expense. Meanwhile I sat there and took it, knowing my time was coming.

"Go on," I said when she suddenly stopped reading.

"Carolyn Fleischower," she said. "I forgot about her."

Hers wasn't one of the names on my list of possible suspects. "What about Carolyn?" I said.

Ruth turned the sausage over and picked up the pages again. "Just something I heard. That she and Whitey Huffer have been carrying on for some time." When I didn't say anything, she said, "Why does that bother you?"

"I've always liked Carolyn Fleischower. That's all."

"You've always liked Claire Huffer, too. Too well to my way of thinking. And she's married to Whitey Huffer."

"Go on," I said, not wanting to discuss it. "Finish the list."

"Raymond Fleischower." Carolyn's brother. "Another possibility."

"Why Raymond?" I asked. His was another name not on my list.

She deliberated a moment, then said, "I've heard he has a drug problem."

"He's always seemed fine around me."

Besides being my dentist, Raymond Fleischower was also my friend. He and his wife, Carla, had been among the few guests at the only party I'd ever thrown in Oakalla. Ruth had been there. So had Rupert and Elvira Roberts. And Clarkie, who turned out to be the life of the party. And Diana who came first and left last, much to Ruth's dismay.

"Raymond's always seemed fine around me, too," Ruth said. "I'm just passing on what I heard." She laid the pages down and began to take up the sausage patties.

"You didn't finish the route," I said.

"What's to finish? Whitey and Claire Huffer are the last ones on the route. If you don't count Larry Stout, Claire's brother."

"I have to count him, Ruth. Particularly since he might have been the one in the hardware with Whitey Huffer last night."

She turned on the oven and set the platter of sausage inside it to keep the sausage warm. "But what does Larry

Stout have that anybody else would want? Besides his land."

"What does Claire Huffer have that anybody else would want, besides her land?" I said.

Ruth gave me a knowing look. I felt my ears burn.

"Besides that," I said.

"Let me think on it."

While I set the table and poured the orange juice, Ruth fried us each a couple eggs in the sausage grease and then fixed a stack of toast. I hadn't been hungry when I came down the stairs, but I managed to eat everything in sight and then drink a second cup of coffee. Ruth seemed preoccupied. She had said little once we started to eat.

"Agree or disagree?" I said, trying to draw her out.

"About what?"

"Amel Pilkin. That he could have knowingly picked up something of value to somebody else on his route Friday?"

"Agree," she said. "I'm just trying to figure out what it could be."

"Let's go ahead a few hours," I said. "To the Corner Bar and Grill. You remember how excited Amel was, so excited that he couldn't make himself understood. It seems to me that Amel knew the value of what he had. Otherwise, why would he be so excited?"

"I was thinking about that, too," she said, shoving her plate to one side. "But it doesn't make sense to me, Garth. None of it does at this point. Except Amel's dead, Rupert's gone, and you're on the firing line. I must be getting old, because that bothers me more than it would have a few years ago."

"Don't talk about getting old," I said. "That's the way Rupert started talking, and the next thing I know, he's left for Texas."

"It's a fact of life, Garth. You can't ignore it. We all grow old sometime."

"True. But I don't have to like it."

8

TWO HOURS LATER, when the sun had risen high enough to make it seem warmer than it was, I got into Jessie and drove southeast of town. Jessie's heater only worked in summer and only then if I didn't need it, but I turned it on anyway. I liked having the cold air blow up my pants leg. In time it felt almost warm.

Up until two years ago, Carolyn Fleischower had lived with her father, Norman Fleischower, on the farm where she was raised. Then Norman Fleischower had died, leaving Carolyn alone on the farm.

I remembered Norman Fleischower as a large florid man with a bulbous nose and creamy white hair, who delighted in racing his go-cart back and forth between floats in Oakalla's annual homecoming parade. A part-time lawyer, a part-time farmer, and a full-time politician who once said he would kiss a snake if it would help elect his man, Norman Fleischower enjoyed his whiskey and enjoyed his life, and wanted you to enjoy it with him. And in the times we'd spent together, mostly at the bar at the Corner Bar and Grill, I honestly could say that I enjoyed life whenever Norman Fleischower was around.

Carolyn Fleischower stood about five feet ten inches tall, had short brown hair, thick ankles, and a pretty face, and like to wear muumuus and sandals. She taught kindergarten in Oakalla, had for the past twenty years, and unlike her father, could have cared less about politics.

"Garth!" she said on answering my knock at her back door. "You caught me at a bad time. I wasn't expecting company."

She wore a thin lavender housecoat and lavender slippers with fuzzy white rabbit on the toe of each of them. She also wore lipstick, eye shadow, and had brushed her hair until it shone. For someone not expecting company, she looked awfully ready for it.

"Do you mind if I come in?" I said. "I'm freezing my tail off out here."

She minded. But she let me in anyway—at least as far as the utility room where she kept her stand-up freezer and her canning jars.

"I'm sorry to bother you," I said, taking off my gloves and stocking cap, and wiggling my toes to make sure they were still there. "But something's come up and I need your help."

She glanced past me and outside to where Jessie was parked. Her eyes said that Jessie was an unwelcome sight. I doubted that her reasons were the same as mine.

"I'll be glad to help you, Garth. But not today. As I said, it's really not a good time."

"It'll only take a minute," I said, happy to feel my toes again. "Amel Pilkin came by here on his route Friday. Or at least he was supposed to. I just wondered what he picked up here."

"Just the usual," she said. She continued to look outside.

"Which is?"

She looked at me. Her big brown eyes showed tears. Apparently I was about to ruin her day.

"Cans and bottles. Stuff like that. Nothing very large. Amel's truck wouldn't hold it." She thought a moment, then said, "Oh, and some of dad's old suits and sport coats that I've had around here forever."

I remembered the sport coat that I'd seen Amel wearing in the Corner Bar and Grill on Friday night. The one that hung to his knees. "Was one of them red plaid? Looked like something out of a best-dressed clown magazine?"

"Yes," she laughed, momentarily herself again. "Dad loved that sport coat more than any other. He used to wear it to tease mother because he knew how much she hated it." Her eyes were teary again. "But after mother died, he quit wearing it altogether."

"When did your mother die?" I thought I remembered her, but I wasn't certain.

"Nearly ten years ago. Not very long after Warren Stout died, if you remember him. He and dad were best buddies, best everything really. After mother and Warren died within just a few months of each other, I think a lot of the fun went out of dad's life." She forced a smile. "But of course dad would never let anyone know that. Hail fellow well met that he was."

Though I knew Norman Fleischower well, I'd only met Warren Stout a couple times. But I remembered him as a small, slight, sardonic man with thin grey hair and the most remarkably clear eyes I'd ever seen.

"I liked your dad," I said. "I don't think he ever met a stranger, or someone he didn't like."

"That was dad," she said. "Politician to the bitter end."

"Was his end all that bitter?" If I remembered right, Norman Fleischower had had a stroke and died in his sleep.

"For me it was," she said, no longer able to hold back her tears. "Because when he died, I lost my best friend."

I let myself out and stood on the back step a moment, surveying the farm. It had no cows, pigs, chickens, dogs, cats, rabbits, goats, guineas, tractors, woodlots, or fences that I could see. What it had were buildings, fields, furrows, foxtail, starlings, and sparrows. I guessed you could still call it a farm.

I got in Jessie and drove southeast right into the sun. I'd only gone a few hundred yards when I met and passed Whitey Huffer's patrol car. Apparently Whitey's mind was

somewhere else because he didn't even slow down but
continued down the road toward Carolyn Fleischower's
farm. I turned around in the next lane and went back the way
I'd come.

Whitey's patrol car wasn't sitting in Carolyn Fleischower's drive, but then I didn't expect it to be. Even he wasn't
that stupid. Neither was I stupid enough to boldly pull in the
drive, and knock on the back door, and ask for him. Instead,
I drove on past the house, parked Jessie along the road,
hopped a ditch, and keeping the barn between the house and
me, went to see what I might learn.

First, I learned that I wasn't really dressed to be out in the
wind, which had begun to pick up now that an army of
ragged grey clouds, scudding across the sky from west to
east, had reached the sun. Second, I learned that Whitey
Huffer's brown-on-brown Plymouth was parked alongside
Carolyn Fleischower's grey-on-blue Chrysler Le Baron in
her otherwise empty machinery shed. Third, I learned that if
you go looking in someone's bedroom window, you'd better
be prepared for what you might see. But fortunately, it was
Carolyn Fleischower standing there in the nude ready to pull
the shade down, instead of Whitey Huffer.

I ducked around the side of the house and headed straight
across the barnyard toward Jessie. At any second I expected
to hear the back door burst open, followed by several rounds
from Whitey Huffer's .44 Magnum. I didn't know if he
could hit me at that range, but I wasn't willing to bet that he
couldn't.

Once I'd rounded the barn without being shot, I slowed to
a jog and concentrated on keeping my footing in the plowed
frozen field. The furrows were deep and uneven and hard to
navigate with big feet and cold toes, but in the end it was a
clod that sent me sprawling.

I rolled over on my back and lay there, watching one
cloud after another scoot across the sky, and wondering why
Carolyn Fleischower hadn't blown the whistle on me.
Embarrassment perhaps had kept her from it. Or discretion.

Or the shock and absurdity of seeing me outside her bedroom window. Whatever her reason, I was grateful to her. Though I had the feeling that in gaining her mercy, I had lost her friendship.

Jessie balked when I tried to start her, and I had to mash her accelerator to the floor and hold it there until she fired. Then she sputtered for several seconds before she decided to go. I slammed her into gear and took off before she had a chance to change her mind.

I didn't have the guts to drive past Carolyn Fleischower's house again, so I went west to the first crossroad and turned north, intending to turn back east at the first opportunity. Though I tried to put it out of my mind, I couldn't shake the sight of seeing Carolyn Fleischower in the buff. She had larger fuller breasts than I ever imagined, and a sleeker firmer body, since most of what I'd mistaken for fat was actually bone.

I envied Whitey Huffer. He had Claire Huffer at home and Carolyn Fleischower on the side, while I had only Ruth at home and nobody on the side—at least nobody that I could call my own.

9

RAYMOND FLEISCHOWER AND his wife, Carla, lived exactly a mile east of his sister on the eastern edge of what was once their farm. Carolyn Fleischower had kept the homeplace and a couple acres around it and sold her half of the 160-acre farm to Claire Huffer and Claire's brother, Larry Stout. Raymond Fleischower had kept twenty acres for himself, built a pond and planted a grove of white pine trees, and then sold what was left to Claire Huffer and Larry Stout.

Raymond and Carla Fleischower lived in a modern red-brick ranch house with their four Labrador retrievers, two cockatoos, and a Russian blue cat named Ivan. Tall, robust, and easygoing, with curly black hair, a black mustache, and deep black friendly eyes, Raymond Fleischower looked like a Swedish version of Tom Selleck. Unlike his father, Raymond wanted nothing to do with politics, and except for his involvement in the Sierra Club and the National Wildlife Federation, was about as apolitical as anyone I'd ever met.

Raymond's wife, Carla, on the other hand, enjoyed a good fight, whether it was with the County Council for not providing an animal shelter in Adams County or with her neighbors for draining their wetlands. Carla packed so much energy into that small brown body of hers that Raymond swore that if you listened closely enough, you could hear her sizzle, like high-voltage line. I had never listened that closely, but I had no reason to doubt him.

I parked Jessie in their stone drive and knocked on their front door. Carla, accompanied by all four of the black Labs, answered it. She wore jeans, a sweatshirt, a blue bandanna in her hair, and the look of someone who didn't want to be bothered. But that's the way Carla Fleischower always looked. As Raymond said about her, she always had her game face on.

"Is Raymond here?" I asked.

"He's down by the pond cutting firewood," she said.

"Thanks. I'll catch him there."

"Is there anything I can help you with?" she said. She didn't seem too anxious for me to talk to Raymond. Rather, she would have preferred for me to talk to her first.

"I was going to ask him if Amel Pilkin came by here Friday afternoon and if Amel picked anything up."

"Why?" she asked sharply. Then she shivered, no doubt from the cold. "I mean why is it any business of yours?"

"You know Amel was found dead in his truck Saturday morning?"

"I heard. I also heard his death was accidental."

"As far as I know it was," I said, wondering why she felt it necessary to remind me of that.

"So?" she said.

"So what?"

"So why is it any business of yours?" she repeated. "We have a sheriff. Why not let him handle the investigation, if you think one is needed."

"Who said anything about an investigation?" I said. "I just asked if Amel Pilkin stopped by here Friday afternoon."

"Sure you did," she said. She stepped back inside the house and closed the door.

I walked the two hundred yards or so back to the pond where Raymond Fleischower was cutting firewood and throwing it into his four-wheel-drive Toyota pickup. Ironically, that same pickup likely would have belonged to Amel

Pilkin one day, since it was Raymond who had given Amel the yellow Toyota pickup in which Amel died.

Raymond at least seemed glad to see me. He shut off the chain saw and took off his glove to shake my hand.

"Long time no see," he said. Some of the sawdust had caught in Raymond's hair. It looked like snow.

"I guess it has been a while," I said. "You need any help?"

"No thanks," he said with a smile. "I like to go at my own pace, if you know what I mean."

I knew what he meant. With someone else there you always felt the need to keep on working, even when you wanted to rest. And with someone else there you hardly ever stopped to pick up a handful of wet sawdust to smell it, or took a long admiring look at the sky, or thanked God for such a beautiful day and the wherewithal to enjoy it.

"So," he said, tossing a chunk of hickory into the bed of the pickup, "what's on your mind?"

"Amel Pilkin is mainly what's on my mind."

He reached down and threw another chunk of hickory into the pickup. "What about Amel?"

"You know they found him dead yesterday morning?"

"I know," he said, losing his smile. "That's one of the reasons I'm out here cutting wood this morning. I'm trying to forget that I'm the one who gave Amel that pickup."

"You can't blame yourself for that," I said. "Amel got a lot of good years out of it. Five by my count."

He looked away, toward the house. "Yeah. Five good years. And one bad night."

A cloud covered the sun. I felt the wind cut all the way through me. "There is a chance that Amel's death wasn't an accident," I said.

He turned my way. I couldn't tell whether he wanted it to be an accident or not. Raymond Fleischower had always been hard to read.

"In what way not an accident?" he asked.

I deliberated on whether to tell him or not. But since I had brought it up, I might as well see it through. "It's possible that somebody hit Amel over the head and then left him there in the pickup to die."

"Who would do that to Amel?" he said, dismissing that thought. "You and I both know he didn't have an enemy in the world."

"At least not until Friday."

Raymond locked both hands behind his lower back and stretched. Then he bent down to fill his chain saw with gas.

"Don't forget the oil," I said, as he pulled the starter cord.

He gave me a questioning look. Either he hadn't heard me or he didn't understand what I was saying.

"The chain-and-bar oil," I said. "It's there at your feet."

The chain-and-bar oil was what lubricated the chain. If you ran out of it before you ran out of gas, your chain would get hot and bind.

"Thanks, Garth," he said. "I must've been thinking about something else."

"Carla said Amel was by here Friday afternoon," I said, fishing for answers. Carla hadn't said that, but her actions had.

"He was," Raymond said. "So what?" He acted defensively, the way Carla had.

"I just wondered what he might have picked up here. If it was anything out of the ordinary."

He shrugged. "You'll have to ask Carla. She was the one who was home at the time. I was at my office."

"I did ask Carla. She didn't seem to want to talk about it."

He shrugged again as if that were Carla's and my problem, then added chain-and-bar oil to the chain saw and tried to start it again without success.

"Did you turn it on?" I asked.

He glanced up at me. He looked as if he wanted to hit me. "No," he said. "I didn't turn it on."

Once he turned it on, the chain saw started on the first pull. I could still hear it running when I pulled out of his drive.

10

CLAIRE AND WHITEY Huffer lived in a two-story red-brick farmhouse back a tree-lined lane that was at least a quarter of a mile long. Their barn, one of the largest in Adams County, sat high on a red stone foundation and was surrounded by three blue steel grain silos, a farrowing house, a self-contained finishing house with its own white silo, a drying bin, a machinery shed, and two corn-cribs.

Their house had a sheer brick face, two steep narrow gables that made me think of ostrich wings, no porch front or back, and was built around a two-room log cabin that if not the oldest, was close to the oldest dwelling in Adams County. A blue spruce, two majestic Norway pines, and a grand old willow grew in the backyard. Several small cedars and the remains of an apple orchard grew out front.

On my way in the lane, I met a grey Mercedes convertible on its way out. I pulled as far over to the right side of the lane as I could without hitting a tree and stopped. The Mercedes, which had two men in topcoats inside it, sped on past me as if I weren't there, taking its share of the lane out of the middle. I wished then that I hadn't stopped. If nothing else, Jessie was big and solid and more than a match for a Mercedes convertible.

Claire Huffer didn't answer when I knocked on her front door, so I went looking for her. She wasn't in either the farrowing house or the finishing house. What was in the farrowing house were several Berkshire sows, some with

large litters of little black pigs and others who were either
very fat or very pregnant. In the finishing house, the hogs
being fattened for market were lying placidly in their little
iron pens, surrounded by everything a hog could want. Too
stuffed to even grunt, they were the embodiment of hog
heaven and the phrase "there's no such thing as a free
lunch."

I finally found Claire Huffer in the barn where she was
throwing down hay for her Holsteins. Up until a few years
ago, she had milked the Holsteins, and the milking parlor
and stanchions were still there in the barn below the
haymow. But now she raised the Holsteins for slaughter.

"Garth!" she said, climbing down from the mow. "What
brings you out here? It's to see me, I hope."

Claire Huffer was forty years old. She had curly orange-
red hair, hazel eyes, a peaches-and-cream complexion, and
a taught wiry body that never seemed to tire. I had never
seen her in anything but jeans or coveralls, and except for
the day that I interviewed her for my article on women
farmers, never had talked to her for more than a few minutes
at a time. But those few times I had been in her company,
I had felt the sparks fly back and forth between us.
Attractive, though not especially charming or beautiful,
Claire Huffer was also bright, clever, bold, and frank. And
for some reason, one I had never examined too closely, I
found that desirable.

I stood back as she jumped from the ladder and landed at
my feet. She wore green coveralls and work boots. I reached
out and picked a piece of hay from her hair.

"I bet I look a mess, don't I?" she said.

"You look fine to me."

We neither one said anything for a moment. I was too
busy counting the rungs of the ladder. She had found
something on the far wall to look at.

"You never answered my question," she said, directing
her gaze at me. "What brings you here?"

I studied her while trying hard not to let her know it. Her

eyes were clear and calm. Her face friendly, eager, and open. She appeared to have nothing to hide.

"I'd be a liar if I said it was just to see you," I said. "I'd be a liar if I said it wasn't to see you. But why I'm here is to ask you some questions about Amel Pilkin."

"Does Whitey know you're here?" she said.

"No. Whitey doesn't know I'm here," I said. I didn't think it was necessary to tell her that probably at that very moment Whitey was humping her best friend.

"I didn't think so," she said. "In fact, if he knew you were here, he might get ugly."

"Most likely."

She smiled. I liked her smile. It was bold and to the point, just like Claire Huffer. "And still here you are."

"In the flesh."

"Then you might as well make yourself useful."

I helped her break the bales and feed the hay to the cattle, who by then were crowding into the barn.

"Would you like coffee?" she said when we finished.

"Now that you asked."

We went into the house through the back door. She took off her insulated coveralls and hung them on a peg just inside the door. She wore jeans and a blue flannel shirt beneath them. I noticed how well her jeans fit her. Grandmother Ryland had said that there was nothing sweeter than a cow's breath on a cold day. But she had never seen Claire Huffer bend over.

"Have you been admiring my butt?" she said.

I felt myself blush. Caught in the act. "Yes."

"I thought so." Her smile was sweet but deadly. "It could have been yours, you know, if you'd played your cards right."

"That's not something I need to hear."

"Don't be silly, Garth," she said, leading the way into the kitchen. "I'm married, remember?" Her face momentarily darkened. "But then that doesn't stop Whitey, does it?"

Though she had invited my comment, I thought it prudent not to make one. But she wouldn't let me off that easily.

"So would you or wouldn't you?" she said, dumping the grounds from her coffeepot and adding fresh coffee.

"Would I or wouldn't I what?"

"Make love to me if you had the chance?" She filled the coffeepot with water and set it on the stove.

"I wouldn't," I said and hoped I meant it.

"Why not?"

"Because you're married."

"And you don't do married women, right?" Her voice was playful, her eyes less so.

"Right. I don't do married women."

"Not even Whitey Huffer's wife?"

"Especially not Whitey Huffer's wife."

"Why? Don't tell me you're afraid of Whitey," she teased, as she turned to light the burner under the coffeepot.

"No, I'm not afraid of Whitey."

Her back was to me as she said, "You should be, you know." Her voice had lost its playfulness.

"So I've heard."

She turned to face me. Her look was somber. So was the rest of her, as if something had drained her high spirits and left her empty.

"I'm serious, Garth. He hates your guts. Any excuse . . . I mean *any* excuse that he can find to hurt or embarrass you in any way, he'll use just like that." She snapped her fingers to show me how fast "just like that" was.

"I believe you," I said.

"And still you're not scared?"

"Not of Whitey," I said.

"Then what does scare you?"

"You," I said in all honesty.

"Do you mind explaining yourself?"

"Sometime perhaps. Not now."

While she went into the bathroom to wash her hands, I

took the opportunity to survey the kitchen. I had been in there for coffee once before, but I still found it as fascinating as I had the first time.

All four walls of the kitchen were the huge, roughhewn timbers of the original log cabin. The ceiling was also the original ceiling. Its nine-inch tall milled beams still had flakes of white paint on them and were studded with square nails and leather straps from which lanterns and utensils had hung at one time.

A big stone fireplace, now cold, sat among the logs opposite me. Stoneware crocks and jugs along with other primitives, including a butter churn and a branding iron, sat on the hearth, the mantel, and on top of all of the cabinets. I imagined that when a fire was burning in the fireplace and bread was baking in the oven, it was about as cozy as a kitchen could be. What I had a hard time imagining was Whitey Huffer and Claire Huffer sitting there in front of the fire together. But I had no trouble imagining Claire Huffer sitting there with me.

Claire returned to the kitchen just in time to turn the fire down under the coffee before it boiled over. Along with washing her hands, she had brushed her hair. Its curls were loose and soft and shiny.

"You owe me an explanation," she said, sitting across from me at the table. "And I won't let you out of here without it. Why are you afraid of me, Garth?"

"I'm afraid that once I loved you, I couldn't stop."

That wasn't the answer she was expecting. She had to look away. "I see," she said. "It's that serious, is it?"

"It's that serious," I said, not trying to hide anything from her. "But it's not something I want to discuss."

"Me either," she said, feeling the sudden need to be doing something, as she rose to check on the coffee. "I was talking about a roll in the hay. Not a lifetime commitment."

"You made a lifetime commitment to Whitey Huffer," I said.

"That's different."

"In what way?"

She reached up and took two coffee mugs from the cabinet. One was black and said "his" on it. The other was yellow and said "hers" on it. She filled the black cup with coffee and set it in front of me. Then without asking, she also set a cream pitcher and a sugar bowl in front of me.

"You take cream and sugar, right?" she said. "A splash of cream and a teaspoon and a half of sugar."

"Right," I said, wondering how she'd remembered. Or more to the point, why she'd bothered to remember.

She filled the yellow cup and brought it with her as she sat back down across from me. "It's different in that Whitey doesn't get in my way, and I don't get in his. I was thirty-seven when I married Whitey, Garth. I wasn't looking for love."

"What were you looking for?"

She shrugged. "Who knows? Maybe just a warm body to snuggle up to at night. Certainly not someone who would expect me to be there for him or who would be there for me. Though," she said with a wistful smile, "it would be nice at times."

I returned her smile. "Do you mind if we change the subject?" I said, knowing where we were headed and unwilling to go there, since I'd been there before with Diana and had the scars to prove it. Sometimes, when you got involved with someone whom you wanted more completely than she wanted you, it didn't matter if she was married or not. In the end, you still ended up alone.

"Fine by me. What do you want to talk about?"

"Amel Pilkin, for starters. I need to know if he came by here Friday afternoon."

"He did. Or at least I think he did. The stuff I had out for him was gone when I got back from town."

I took a sip of my coffee. It was nearly as good as Ruth's, and Ruth made the best coffee around. "Do you remember if you had anything unusual in your trash this time?" I asked.

"In what way unusual?"

"Out of the ordinary."

She thought it over. "No. It was mostly cans and bottles, stuff like that. The big things we haul out to our dump in back."

I'd asked the questions I'd come to ask, but I still wasn't ready to leave. It was cold outside, warm in there.

"Carolyn Fleischower said that your father and her father used to be best friends," I said for something to say.

"When did you talk to Carolyn?" she said.

"Earlier this morning."

"Was Whitey there yet?"

The question caught me off guard. I didn't know how to answer it. "Was he supposed to be there?" I said.

"Come off it, Garth," she admonished me. "Don't tell me you're the only one in Adams who doesn't know my husband is screwing my best friend."

"No. I didn't know," I said. "And no, he wasn't there yet."

"Good thing for you."

"Yes. Good thing for me."

She took a drink of her coffee. She was trying hard to be above it all but not succeeding very well. "What did you say about my father?"

"I said that he and Norman Fleischower were best friends."

"They were," she agreed. "Best friends, best fishing-buddies, best drinking-buddies, best everything, you name it. Mutt and Jeff. That's what people used to call them because daddy was so small and quiet and Norman was such a big windbag. But even though they didn't look or act a thing alike, they each had one all-consuming passion, which was life itself. Both were full of it and lived it to the fullest. Too bad they each didn't have longer to enjoy it." She forced a smile, as if surprised at herself for saying so much. "Now aren't you sorry you asked?"

"No," I said. "I'm sorry I didn't get the chance to know your father better."

"So am I, Garth. I think you would have liked daddy. And I know he would have liked you."

We finished our coffee and walked to the back door where Claire took her coveralls from the peg and put them on again. While she was doing that, I took the .22 Winchester carbine down from above the door and looking through its infrared scope, drew a bead on Jessie. "Is this thing loaded?" I asked.

"Always," she said. "We have a lot of trouble with coyotes out here." She looked grim. "And jackals."

"Jackals?"

"It's a private joke."

"That reminds me," I said, being very careful as I hung the Winchester back above the door. "I met a couple of men in a grey Mercedes convertible as I was coming up the lane. They weren't by any chance from Bench-Mart, were they?"

"Yes," she said, still looking grim. "How did you know?"

"A lucky guess. How are things going with them anyway? I hear you're about to close on the deal."

She yanked so hard on her zipper that I was afraid she was going to tear it off. "We close in another month. If all goes well."

"Then why aren't you happier about it?"

"Because I didn't want to sell the land in the first place. It's Whitey's doings, not mine."

"Then why go along with it?"

"Circumstances," she said.

"What kind of circumstances?"

"The kind I don't want to talk about." She put her hand to my face and held it there. For a hand that was used for driving tractors, bucking bales, and pulling calves, it was extraordinarily soft. "Times are hard on the farm, Garth. Or haven't you heard?"

I put my right arm around her, squeezed her hard, and left. If I'd stayed any longer, I wouldn't have gone.

11

IN SOME WAYS Larry Stout, Claire Huffer's brother and Warren Stout's son, reminded me of his father. He was small and slender like his father, and at forty-five his thin brown hair had already started to turn grey. Like his father, he didn't volunteer much information about himself or anything else, but when he did speak, he spoke with authority and people listened. Unlike his father, he didn't yet seem embittered with life that had somehow betrayed him. But then Larry Stout wasn't dying of cancer, as his father had been when I knew him.

Larry Stout live alone in a small white frame tenant house on the southeast corner of his and his sister's two thousand acre farm. He had never married, and as the safe money said around Oakalla, it was a pretty sure bet that he never would marry. For companionship, he had a collie named Buster Brown, who went just about everywhere with Larry, and on warmer days could be seen riding through Oakalla with his head out the window of Larry's green Ford pickup, barking at everything in sight.

But Larry Stout and Buster Brown were not at home. I went to all the places where I thought they might be and didn't find them there, either. Since I was in the neighborhood and since Ruth's Sunday dinner wouldn't be ready for another hour, I decided to go to Pilkin's Knob to see if I'd overlooked anything the day before. There I found Larry Stout's pickup parked in Amel Pilkin's drive.

Buster Brown came around the corner of the house and started barking at me. Larry Stout soon followed him. I stayed in Jessie. I didn't think Buster Brown would bite me, but he might if he thought Larry was in danger.

"What are you doing here?" Larry said.

"I was just going to ask you the same thing."

Buster Brown jumped up on Jessie to get a closer look at me. I scratched his chin, then gently lifted his paws off of Jessie's door. He dropped to the ground. Jessie didn't like anything leaning on her, dogs included.

"Buster, come here," Larry said, slapping his leg.

When Buster Brown obeyed, and I never had known him not to obey Larry, Larry picked him up, set him in the pickup, and closed the door on him. Buster Brown took it all in stride, however, and sat there calmly with his long nose pressed to the glass.

"Crazy dog," Larry said with affection. "But I don't know what I would do without him."

Larry walked up to Jessie and looked inside, but he didn't say anything. I didn't know quite what to say either, so I kept quiet. Then Larry took a pack of Camels out of the pocket of his grey coveralls and offered me one. When I shook my head no, he put a cigarette into his mouth, bent down and away from the wind, and lighted it.

"Kind of cold out here today," he said.

"I noticed that."

"You plan on staying long?" The question seemed innocent enough, but I wondered what his purpose was in asking it.

"Not long."

He turned away from the wind to relight his cigarette. "Me either. In fact, I was just about to leave."

"Did you find what you were looking for?"

He took the cigarette out of his mouth and exhaled a puff of smoke. Immediately the wind whisked the smoke away. "Who said I was looking for anything," he said, putting the cigarette back in his mouth.

"Then this is a social call?" It was possible, though not likely, that he hadn't heard that Amel was dead.

"It's a farewell, Garth," he said. "And a good riddance." He got into his pickup, pushed Buster Brown to the other side, and drove away.

On his way down from Pilkin's Knob, he met another vehicle on its way up. They stopped side by side in the middle of Bear Hollow Road. Though I couldn't see it clearly, the vehicle facing me looked a lot like Raymond Fleischower's black Toyota pickup.

Then the other pickup backed up, staying just ahead of Larry, as Larry went forward, screening my view. When they'd gone about a hundred yards, the other pickup turned around and went the other way with Larry's pickup following it. I got out of Jessie and went on into the house.

Someone had wrecked the place. He had opened every drawer in Amel's house and dumped its contents. He had opened Amel's ice chest and emptied it, as ice, bread, and bologna lay in one big frozen lump on the floor. He had taken the cushions from Amel's couch and slit their lining, slit open Amel's mattress and dug out its stuffing, turned his table and chairs upside down. He had even taken the ashes from Amel's stove and dumped them on the floor where, it appeared, he had sifted through them in his search for whatever it was he was looking for.

After what I'd seen in the house, I fully expected what I found in Amel's storage shed. All his barrels had been overturned, and their contents spread over the dirt floor, until I couldn't move without stepping in someone's garbage. I didn't bother to go through it piece by piece. I doubted that I would find anything.

Carolyn Fleischower had driven her Chrysler Le Baron halfway up Pilkin's Knob before she saw Jessie parked there. In her haste to turn around, she got her front wheels off the road and into the ditch. Even though frozen on top, the ground there in the ditch was soft beneath the crust, like the soft center of a fruit pie. Carolyn Fleischower sat there spinning her wheels.

I got in Jessie and drove down to where she was stuck. She stayed inside her car and wouldn't look at me until I tapped on her window. She was wearing more clothes than the last time I'd seen her. But her makeup was all but gone.

"I have a chain in the trunk," I said. "Hang on a minute, and I'll pull you out."

"Don't bother," she said. "I don't accept help from peeping toms."

I didn't say anything. I just stood there in the cold, waiting for her to make the next move.

"You heard me," she said angrily. "Go on down the road."

"Would it help to say that I was sorry?"

"Not much." Then she rolled down her window. "Whatever possessed you anyway? Just answer me that."

"I had to know what Whitey was doing there."

"Why? Why is it any business of yours?"

I nodded toward the house on Pilkin's Knob. "Why is Amel Pilkin suddenly an interest of yours? And don't tell me you got lost on the way to town either. Did Whitey send you here?"

"No!" she said. "I'm here on my own. If Whitey knew I was here, he wouldn't like it."

"Than let me rephrase my question. Are you here on Whitey's behalf?"

"What if I am?" she said. "Which I'm not."

Carolyn Fleischower made a poor liar. She couldn't look me in the eye as she did it, the way the pros did.

"If you are here on Whitey's behalf," I said, "then you should know why I was looking in your bedroom window this morning. Even if you aren't here on Whitey's behalf, you still should know why."

"That's not true," she said. "Not a word of it's true." She gunned her engine, throwing mud all over her car and me. Then she started to cry.

I got the chain out of Jessie's trunk, hooked it to the Le

Baron's frame, and coaxed Jessie downhill until the chain tightened. Then I went to talk to Carolyn Fleischower.

"Put it in reverse," I said. "And try not to spin your tires."

I got back in Jessie, gave her the gas, and slowly crept forward down the hill. To my relief, Carolyn Fleischower did exactly as I'd asked, and I soon had her out of the ditch. But as soon as I unfastened the chain from the Le Baron, she sped up the hill to Pilkin's Knob, turned around, and threw gravel all over Jessie and me on her way past. With nothing more to do there, I went home.

12

FOR SUNDAY DINNER Ruth had fixed beef brisket, boiled cabbage, fried potatoes and onions, and tapioca for dessert. I got home with just time to change clothes before I sat down to eat.

Afterwards, we sat at the dining room table, drinking coffee. We used the dining room once a week and that was for Sunday dinner. Then we also used the good silver, the good china, and the linen napkins and tablecloth. The rest of the time we ate off of Fiestaware in the kitchen.

"So what do you do now?" Ruth asked.

During dinner I had told her how my morning had gone. What I hadn't told her was how hard it was to leave Claire Huffer and how good Carolyn Fleischower looked in the buff.

"I don't know that I do anything," I said. "I'm about to turn things over to you."

"Why don't you just forget about it?" she suggested.

"Could you? Knowing what I know."

She picked up her coffee cup and set it back down again on its saucer. It was always strange to see her using a china cup instead of the heavy ironstone one she usually drank from. For one meal a week, we were proper. The rest of the time, we were ourselves.

"That's just it, Garth. You don't know anything more than when you started. At least about Amel Pilkin and why he died."

"That's where you come in," I said. "I need some background on him. Him and everyone else involved."

"Why?" she said, not rising to the bait as I hoped she would.

"Why not?" I answered.

She sighed in resignation. She knew me well enough to know that even without her help, I wouldn't stop until I got to the bottom of things. Something in me wouldn't let me stop, though I had yet to discover what that something in me was.

"What is it you want to know, Garth?"

"I want to know who Amel's parents were and why he ended up on Pilkin's Knob in a house with no electricity, no insulation, and no running water. And why someone would trash that house for no apparent reason."

Ruth picked up her china cup and drank from it this time. "He ended up on Pilkin's Knob because that's where he started out some forty years ago. His mother was Lena Pilkin, a pretty, but simpleminded girl who wasn't too careful about the company she kept. His father could have been any of the young men around Oakalla at the time."

"So in truth he never had a father."

"Not to speak of. Though Amel's mother did come into some money shortly before or shortly after Amel was born. Some of us around here believe that came from his father."

"How much money?"

She gave me a look that said what do you want for nothing. "I have no idea. She spent it so fast that no one could keep track of it. Soon she was right back where she started—with nothing."

"So in effect, she squandered Amel's inheritance."

"If you want to look at it that way. I see it as squandering her own. You have to remember that the money was given to her, Garth. Not Amel."

"It amounts to the same thing," I argued.

"If you want to split hairs."

I looked out our south window right at the cloud that had

just covered the sun. Fall through early spring, the dining room was always the brightest room in the house. That is, when the sun shone.

"What about Warren Stout and Norman Fleischower?" I said. "Were they as good friends as everyone says they were?"

"Yes. They were best friends from childhood up until the day Warren died. And it was Warren who sold Norman that farm where Norman's children were raised, which they sold back to Warren's children after Norman died." She drank the rest of her coffee and went into the kitchen to refill her cup and mine. "As for Warren's and Norman's children, you probably know as much about them as I do."

"Not about Whitey Huffer," I said.

"That's one I can't help you with," she said, returning to her chair. "Whitey Huffer's a Johnny-come-lately to Oakalla. He lived most of his life in Madison before moving here a few years ago."

Where he'd met Claire at a farm progress show, or so I'd been told, and married her a few months later. My question was, what was Whitey Huffer doing at a farm progress show? He was no more a farmer than I was. My answer was he was probably there trolling for Claire Huffer.

Ruth noticed that I wasn't saying anything. "What's the matter, cat got your tongue?" she said.

I smiled inwardly. Grandmother Ryland always used to ask me that when, as a kid, I'd lapse into silence. Ruth and Grandmother Ryland had that in common. Neither one liked to watch me think for very long. Maybe it took me too far away from them.

"I was just thinking about what Claire Huffer told me earlier today," I said. "About her reason for selling the land to Bench-Mart. She indicated to me that it was really Whitey's idea and not hers, because, in her words, 'times are hard on the farm.' Have you heard anything about them being in financial trouble?"

"No," she said. "I haven't."

"Do you suppose you could see if there's anything to it?"

"If you will tell me why it's necessary "

"When I was driving in Claire Huffer's lane today, I met a grey Mercedes convertible on its way out. At first I thought it might belong to the people from Bench-Mart. I'm not sure now."

"Why not?"

A car headed south sped by the house, soon followed by another speeding car. I wondered what was up until I heard the fire siren. I went to the window and looked south in the direction the cars had gone. But I didn't see smoke anywhere.

"For one thing," I said, still standing at the dining room window, "I'm not sure that's the way the Bench-Mart people would do business, going to Claire's farm like that without her brother being there. For another thing, she called them jackals, or at least I think that's who she was referring to. I don't think she would call the Bench-Mart people jackals."

"Unlike you," Ruth was quick to point out.

"Unlike me."

"Okay, I'll look into it for you," she said.

"Thanks, Ruth. I appreciate it."

She went to the back door to look for the fire while I went to the front door, but neither one of us could see it. So I began to clear the dining room table while she began to run the dishwater.

"In the meantime, what do you plan to do about Claire Huffer?" she asked.

The question came right out of the blue and caught me off guard. "I don't plan to do anything about her. Why?"

"Just asking," she said.

The phone rang. I hurried to answer it before Ruth could zero in on me.

"Garth Ryland here," I said.

"Chief Deputy Clark here," Clarkie answered. "Do you want to take a ride with me?"

"Where?"

"Pilkin's Knob. The whole place is on fire."

It took me a moment before I could answer. "Sure, Clarkie. I'll be waiting at the door."

"What's wrong?" Ruth asked after I'd hung up.

I told her.

She put a glass into the dishwater and began to wash it. With Ruth, the order was always glasses first, then cups, saucers, plates, silverware, and pots and pans. When I washed dishes, I took them in whatever order they came and piled them wherever I could find room. Which explained why, whenever Ruth was around, she washed and I dried.

Then she said, "I was wrong, Garth. You couldn't forget about Amel Pilkin, even if you wanted to."

Clarkie picked me up in his patrol car, and we drove out Bear Hollow Road toward Pilkin's Knob. But we couldn't get within a quarter mile of the place for all of the cars parked in and along the road. A Sunday afternoon fire was big doings in Oakalla, particularly since the Packers were on the West Coast and wouldn't play until three.

"What do you want to do," Clarkie said, "park it and walk?"

"Do we have any other choice?"

At Pilkin's Knob, firemen and spectators alike stood in a loose ring around Amel's buildings, watching them burn. To keep the fire from spreading to the nearby woods, the firemen kept the ground saturated with water and then knocked down the flames whenever they got too high. But the buildings themselves, including Amel's house, storage shed, and woodhouse, had already been given up for lost.

Claire Huffer and Larry Stout stood several feet apart, but each was a mirror image of the other. Both seemed fascinated by, yet indifferent to, the fire, as if it did not touch them personally. Both watched it stoically, dispassionately, like a horse at a hanging.

Carolyn Fleischower, on the other hand, seemed horrified by it, and she kept looking at Whitey Huffer and he at her as if for reassurance. Raymond and Carla Fleischower held on to each other as they watched the fire, until, when she could no longer bear to watch, Carla buried her face in Raymond's chest.

Orville Goodnight was the first spectator to leave the fire. He walked past Clarkie and me without seeming to see either one of us and got into his new Chevy pickup, which, except for the fire trucks, was the vehicle closest to the fire. Tooting his horn the whole way down from Pilkin's Knob, Orville made his way through the latecomers along Bear Hollow Road toward the sanctity of his own lane.

Others began to leave, two at a time, then in one steady stream until finally Clarkie, Larry Stout, a few of the volunteer firemen, and I were the only ones left. "Where's Buster Brown?" I asked Larry, who seemed intent on watching Amel's house burn down to its last timber.

"I had to leave him at home," Larry said. "He doesn't like fire."

"Neither do I. Not this kind."

He shrugged as if to say what did it matter. Then he climbed into his green Ford pickup and left.

When the fire had burned itself to ashes, I helped the remaining firemen roll the water out of the hoses so they wouldn't freeze and put the hoses on the trucks. "What do you think?" I asked Danny Palmer, who, along with owning the Marathon service station, was Oakalla's volunteer fire chief.

"About what?" he said. Danny's face was smudged with soot, and he had a small cut over his right eye.

"The fire. Was it arson or not?"

"Ask me tomorrow," he said. "After I've had a chance to shift through the ashes."

"Then tell me this if you can. Who called in the fire?"

He took off his helmet and gloves and wiped the sweat from his forehead, smearing the soot as he did. "I don't know who called the fire in," he said. "Sniffy, do you remember?"

His face white, his eyes closed, Sniffy Smith sat on the

running board of one of the fire trucks, looking like a dead man. For years Sniffy had complained to Danny that he had always wanted to be a volunteer fireman. So a couple months ago, Danny had made him one—not only a volunteer fireman, but assistant chief.

Sniffy opened his eyes. He wasn't quite as dead as he looked. "No. I don't know," he said curtly. "And I don't much care, either."

"You're the one who took the call," Danny said.

Sniffy sat without moving, staring at us. "I know that I took the call. He didn't give his name. He just said that there was a fire on Pilkin's Knob."

"Could it have been Orville Goodnight who called the fire in?" I said.

Sniffy slowly rose from the running board of the fire truck. "Could have been," he said. "Come to think of it, it did sound like Orville's voice." He opened the door of the fire truck, climbed up onto the running board, and fell across the seat where he lay without moving. With a wink and a grin, Danny moved Sniffy the rest of the way into the cab and closed the door behind him.

Clarkie and I walked the quarter mile back to his patrol car, then drove up the lane to Orville Goodnight's house. Orville lived in a neat two-story white frame farmhouse that was surrounded by a wide rolling yard and several large sugar maple trees that Orville tapped every March for maple syrup. Orville's white house and red barn always appeared freshly painted, as did the white board fence that lined his lane on both sides. And his herd of Holsteins, before he sold them for slaughter a few years ago, always reminded me of grandmother's Guernseys, the way they looked so fat, sleek, and contented.

Orville stood with his back to us, filling his pickup with gas from his pump. Apparently he hadn't heard us coming. When he turned around to hang up the hose, his mouth flew open in surprise. But he recovered quickly.

"You might as well stay inside that patrol car," he said to

me after hanging up the hose. "I've got nothing to say to you, or that fat, puffed-up, poor excuse for a deputy in there with you."

Clarkie put a white knuckle grip on the wheel but said nothing. I admired his restraint under fire.

"Have it your way, Orville," I said. "But you can either talk to us or talk to the fire marshal tomorrow."

"About what?" He put the gas cap back on his pickup and walked over to me.

"The fire you called in earlier today."

Orville studied me. He had the reputation of being one of the best poker players around Oakalla, so he would know when someone was bluffing.

"Who says I called the fire in?" he said.

"Sniffy Smith."

"Then he's a liar."

"I don't think so, Orville."

"My word against his," he said. "Who's the fire marshal going to believe?"

"That depends on the fire marshal."

"You mean his politics."

"I mean his character."

Orville smiled at me. He now knew he held the winning hand. "Shoot, Garth, what does that have to do with anything? If a man had character, he wouldn't be a politician in the first place. He'd be a farmer or a mechanic or a captain of industry, something where he could be his own boss and not depend on his popularity to keep his job." He reached up and grabbed his coveralls with both hands like a pair of suspenders. "Besides that, I helped get the man elected. So how do you like them apples?"

"The state fire marshal is appointed, Orville."

"Appointed then," he said, not giving any ground. "Hell, two-thirds of the politicians in this state owe me a favor. He's more than likely one of them."

"Who are you protecting, Orville? I know you didn't set that fire. But I bet you know who did."

"Says who?" he said, looking guilty as charged. "Why couldn't I have seen the fire from my place and called it in? I'm not saying that's the way it happened, because it didn't, but why couldn't it have happened that way?"

"It could have happened that way, you dried-up old fart, but it didn't," Clarkie said. "Otherwise, you wouldn't be standing here in the cold, giving us the runaround."

Unknown to me, Clarkie had been simmering the whole time we were there, until he finally boiled over. So much for restraint under fire.

Orville Goodnight never said another word. He pushed himself away from the patrol car and walked across his yard into his house.

"Thanks, Clarkie," I said. "Your timing was perfect."

Clarkie pounded the steering wheel in frustration. "Why do I always have to screw things up? Once, just once, I'd like to do something right. Is that too much to ask?"

"You do a lot of things right, Clarkie," I said. "So don't be too hard on yourself."

"That's what Sheriff Roberts always said. But I'm not sure I believe you any more than I did him."

I thought about Rupert Roberts and wondered if he and Elvira were to El Paso yet. He was getting close by now, if not already there. I wondered, too, if he knew how much I already missed him.

"Your day will come, Clarkie," I said. "All of us get at least one chance in life to be a hero."

"Yeah," he said, not convinced. "And I'll probably screw mine up."

I didn't say anything more because I couldn't be sure that Clarkie wasn't right.

13

I ROSE EARLY the next morning, ate a bowl of Grape-Nuts, drank a glass of orange juice, and arrived at the Marathon shortly after six where I poured myself a cup of coffee and sat down on a plastic chair to drink it. Danny Palmer was the only one in the Marathon. Sniffy Smith had yet to make his appearance.

"Where's Sniffy?" I asked Danny.

"Home nursing his wounds, I imagine. He said on our way home last night that he was too old to be a fireman, that he was sorry now that he'd ever said anything to me."

"Do you think he'll quit?"

Danny smiled. "Over his dead body. He likes to ride the fire truck too well for that."

"And fight fires?"

Danny's smile broadened. "Maybe not as well." Then his smile began to fade. "But then, who does?"

I waited while he counted the change in each drawer to make sure it was exact. Then I waited while he pumped gas for a couple of customers. When he came back into the station again, he was blowing on his hands to warm them.

"It's a bit nippy out there this morning," he said.

"So I've noticed." I finished my coffee, then wadded up my cup and threw it at the barrel in the corner. Two points. "What did you find out about the fire?" I said.

Danny poured himself a cup of coffee and set it on his desk, knowing that he would never get the chance to drink it before it got cold. "It's hard to say, Garth, without calling in the experts, just what I did find out. As fast as the place went up, I'd say it probably had help. The fact that I found a five-gallon gas can on the scene doesn't change my mind any."

"Where did you find it?"

"Inside the shed where Amel stored his trash."

"There wasn't one in there earlier yesterday."

"Imagine that," he said on his way out the door to wait on another customer.

"I wonder why they used gas," I said on his return, "when Amel had a drum of kerosene lying there in his woodshed."

The question didn't intrigue Danny as much as it did me. "We don't know that they didn't use kerosene. We don't even know they used gas."

"Good point," I said. "So maybe we should find out."

He sighed, not wanting to bother on a Monday morning. "I'll give the state fire marshal a call the first chance I get."

"I'd appreciate it." I stood and stretched, briefly postponing my journey out into the cold. "So will Amel."

I walked along Gas Line Road under lavender clouds and a light blue sky. The sun wasn't yet up when I arrived at my office, but by the time I fixed myself a cup of instant coffee and sat down at my desk to drink it, the sun had just peeked over the horizon.

I loved my desk more than anything else in my office, and that included a lot of my favorite mementos. Solid oak and at least five feet long by three feet deep, it had once sat in my father's dairy back in Godfrey, Indiana—it and the swivel chair in which I sat. They had sat in the boiler room right next to the coal furnace. After a hard day's sledding, I used to lean back in the chair with my red bare feet on the desk, while my gloves, boots, and socks dried. Warm and secure, like my childhood itself, the desk always gave me something to lean on when the going got tough.

Whitey Huffer stormed into my office. "Get up," he shouted.

"Why?"

"Because I'm going to kick the living shit out of you. Now get up!"

He didn't have his gun drawn, but I figured that would be his next move if I made any wrong moves. I kept my feet on top of my desk and tried to sit as still as possible.

"That wouldn't be wise, Whitey," I said. "To kick the living shit out of me. You're on duty and in uniform. You might lose your job, and we wouldn't want that."

His face and ears were beet red. I couldn't see his hands because of his calfskin gloves, but I bet they were red with rage, too. "You're a chickenshit, that's what you are, Ryland. You'll kick a man in the balls when he's not looking and mess around with his wife behind his back, but when he calls you on it, you threaten him with his job. We had a name for people like you where I grew up. They were called pussies."

I felt my own ears start to burn a little. "Where did you grow up, Whitey? Did you have a childhood, or did your parents find you in a zoo somewhere?"

"Get up! God damn it," he said, unstrapping his gun and holster. "Get up or I'll take you out right there. I swear I will."

"I'm not going to fight you in here, Whitey. Too many things I value might get broken."

"Then let's step outside."

"For everyone in Oakalla to see? How smart is that, Whitey, for either one of us?"

"Then name your time and place."

The phone rang, as it always did at seven-thirty on a Monday morning. It was Sadie Jenkins, one of my sources, calling to catch me up on all of the "news." I let it ring.

But Whitey Huffer couldn't ignore the phone, even if I could. "Answer it, damn it," he said.

I raised the receiver off of the cradle then set it back down again. Five seconds later the phone rang again. This time I took the receiver off the hook and put it on the desk, but then the phone began to beep loudly.

"Shit!" he said in frustration.

"What'll it be?" I said. "Do I talk to Sadie Jenkins, or do we let the phone beep?"

He put his gun and holster back on. "Do whatever you like. But we have a date Saturday night. If you don't find me, I'll find you."

I set the receiver back on its cradle. If I knew Sadie Jenkins, she was already out the door and on her way to my office.

"Do you mind telling me what it is we'll be fighting about?" I said. "Except that I don't like you and you don't like me."

"You know damn good well what it's about," he said, losing some of his steam. "I know you were out to my house yesterday. So don't try to deny it."

"I won't deny it," I said, wondering how he knew. "But I was there on business. Not for the reason you think."

"What business do you have with my wife? That's what I want to know," he said. By now he looked more hurt than angry. But I wouldn't let myself feel sorry for him.

"I'm trying to find out why Amel Pilkin was killed." I told him the truth to see how he would take it.

"He wasn't killed, God damn it," he said. "His truck quit on him, he got cold and turned on his engine, he fell asleep, and he died. It's that simple." He seemed sincere, but I wasn't buying it. "That's what I say. That's what the coroner says. That's the way it is," he concluded.

"But is it the truth?" I asked.

"*Yes*, it's the truth," he yelled. "What did I just get through telling you?"

"Then how do you explain the knot on the back of Amel Pilkin's head?"

"I don't have to explain the knot on the back of Amel Pilkin's head."

"Somebody does. Also Amel smelled like peach brandy,

but hardly had a drop of it in his blood. What did Amel do, pour the brandy on himself and then knock himself out with the bottle?"

Whitey started to say something then changed his mind. Instead, he walked to my office door where he turned around and said, "Saturday night, Ryland. You and me. Don't forget."

I picked up a stack of ads and started looking through them. "I won't forget."

"And another thing. Stay away from my wife. If I hear you've been anywhere near her, I'm not going to wait for Saturday night."

I looked up at him. Whitey Huffer meant what he said. I had no intention of seeing Claire Huffer again, but I hated to give him the last word.

"If it works out that way," I said.

Whitey didn't get a chance to respond. Sadie Jenkins shoved him out of the way on her way into my office. Of the two of them, I would rather have faced Whitey Huffer.

14

THE NEXT FRIDAY evening, Ruth and I sat in the barroom of the Corner Bar and Grill in exactly the same booth that we had been sitting in the week before when Amel Pilkin had tried to tell me something that I couldn't understand. I had spent my week, as I spent nearly every other week, working on the *Oakalla Reporter* from early in the morning until late at night. Ruth had spent her week, as she spent nearly every other week, cooking, shopping, cleaning, and giving me advice on everything from the writing of my syndicated column to the cut of my hair.

On Monday afternoon, a van from the University of Wisconsin had come for Amel Pilkin's body and taken it away.

On Tuesday the state fire marshal had come with his crew, examined the ruins on Pilkin's Knob, and left with the promise that he would report to Danny Palmer the next day. When he failed to report to Danny the next day, or the day following, Danny called the state fire marshal's office where he got put on hold. Indefinitely.

On Wednesday Claire Huffer had called me at my office to ask me what I'd been up to and why hadn't I been out to see her again. I said that I'd been very busy working on the *Oakalla Reporter,* when I wasn't hiding from her husband, but that I'd be out the sixth week in February. She laughed and called me a coward. What she couldn't know was that I felt like one.

On Thursday another Arctic cold front had drifted down out of Canada, brought a few flurries of snow, and moved on south. The forecast for the weekend ahead was for more of the same.

At 2 a.m. Friday the *Oakalla Reporter* had gone to press, and by Friday noon it had been delivered by mail to just about everyone in and around Oakalla, which is one of the advantages of living in a small town and having same-day delivery. Friday at five, Ruth had called me at my office to tell me that if I wanted supper at home, I'd have to cook it myself. So Friday at six, we had met at the Corner Bar and Grill.

Ruth ordered a Leinenkugels and a New York strip steak, well done. I ordered a Leinenkugels and french-fried shrimp. We agreed to flip a coin at the end of the meal to see who would pay for it.

"So what is it that you wanted to tell me?" I asked Ruth. Along with her news about supper, she also had said she had some other news for me.

"It can wait until we have our beer."

"If you say so."

Hiram brought us each a draft of Leinenkugels. Thirsty after a long day in my office, following a long night at my office, I drank most of mine in one swallow. Ruth gave me a questioning look, like the one my mother used to give me when I'd reach clear across the table to stab a piece of meat.

"I'm thirsty. That's all," I said. I finished the rest of my Leinenkugels with my next swallow.

"I didn't say anything."

I ordered another Leinenkugels and drank this one more slowly. "Go on," I said. "While we have time, why don't you tell me what you have for me?"

"It's what I don't have for you that counts," she said. "You remember that Claire Huffer told you that she and her brother were in some kind of trouble with their farm? Well, if they are, that's news to the people in the know around here."

I wished then that I hadn't drunk my first draft of beer so quickly. I wanted to think about what she'd said, but my mind wouldn't focus. "Just what are you saying, Ruth?" Maybe she would do my thinking for me.

"I'm saying just what I said. Claire Huffer and Larry Stout aren't in trouble with their farm. If anything, they're doing better than ninety-nine percent of the other farmers around here."

"But Claire indicated they were in some kind of trouble," I said, still unwilling to believe Ruth. "That's why they had to sell that forty acres to Bench-Mart."

The look Ruth gave me was unusually harsh, even for her, who had been known to cow muggers and pit bulls alike with just a glance. "Then she lied to you, Garth. That's the long and short of it."

"Why would she lie to me?" I said. "She had no reason to. At least not about that."

"Maybe she's covering up for somebody," Ruth suggested.

"Who?" I wanted to think straight but couldn't. The Leinenkugels and my feelings for Claire Huffer kept getting in the way.

"Maybe her husband. Maybe her brother. Maybe even herself. I don't know, Garth. All I know is that she lied to you."

"Why does that please you?" I said in anger.

She stared at me. I stared right back. "It doesn't please or not please me," she said. "You asked me to do something for you and I did it. What you decide to do about it is your concern, not mine."

"You don't like Claire Huffer, do you?"

She sighed. I'd heard that sigh before. It meant that she was running out of patience with me. "Garth, it's just like with Diana. I don't have any feelings about the woman one way or another. But I do about the fact that she's married and that she married so late in life. She strikes me as a woman who looks out for herself, not a woman who needs looking after."

"You look after yourself," I argued. "If there ever was a woman who looks after herself, it's you."

"I said who looks out *for* herself, not after herself. There's a difference."

I stared dumbly at her. What she had just said made no impression on me. "Then why did she marry Whitey Huffer?"

"Because he's the same way, Garth," she said as if it were obvious to everyone but me. "Look, everyone knows Whitey moves from one woman to the next, cheating on Claire every chance he gets. When you think about it, how well can he like women the way he treats them? It's a tradeoff in my opinion. He gets to use her house and money. She gets to use his . . ." She stopped. I hadn't seen her turn quite that shade of red before. "Anyway, you get the picture."

Clarkie came into the barroom. When I first had seen the pants of his uniform beneath the swinging door, I had mistaken him for Whitey Huffer and thought here we go again.

"Garth," he said. "I've been looking all over town for you."

"Now you've found me." I slid over in the booth to make room for him. "Have a seat."

He shook his head no. "I can't stay," he said. "I'm on my way home now to run something through my computer. I stopped by to ask if you wanted to come along."

"Can it wait until after I've eaten?" I could smell the shrimp, which sat at the kitchen window, waiting to be delivered to me.

Clarkie sat down beside me. "Maybe. If you eat fast."

While I ate, he told me what had happened. Terry and Bobby Banner, two brothers who owned and operated the Banner Sawmill in the west end of Oakalla, had been coon hunting around Hidden Quarry, south of town, when they saw their lights reflect off something shiny. At first they thought it was an animal's eyes, perhaps a coon since it was so near the water, but on closer inspection they discovered a van lodged on some rocks at the water's edge. The van was at least thirty feet down from the rim of the quarry, but Clarkie had managed to get its license plate number and was now on his way home to run it through his computer.

"Done," I said to Clarkie, handing Ruth the check.

"I thought we were going to flip for it."

I took a nickel out of my pocket and flipped it. "Call it."

"Heads," Ruth said.

I caught the nickel and slapped it down on my wrist without looking at it. "Tails."

Ruth glared at me but said nothing.

"The nickel came up heads, Garth," Clarkie said to me on our way out of the Corner Bar and Grill.

"Just don't tell Ruth that."

"I think she already knows."

Clarkie lived in a small white bungalow on the south side of West Street and cant corner to Oakalla's city building. Inside the house were a kitchen, utility room, living room, bathroom, and two bedrooms. Clarkie slept in one of the bedrooms and kept his computer and other electronic equipment in the other one.

I stood in the doorway while Clarkie sat down at his computer. Besides the computer and printer, he had a police scanner, CB radio, and ham radio in there, along with a weather instrument that registered the barometer reading and wind speed and direction. Clarkie said that he could spend days in there at a time and never get bored. I could spend about five minutes.

Clarkie read what was up on the computer screen to me. "The van was stolen from the University of Wisconsin at Madison sometime between twenty-four hundred hours last Sunday and eight hundred hours on Monday."

"Early Monday morning in other words," I said. "Which would make it a day after the fire on Pilkin's Knob."

Clarkie gave me a questioning look, as if I were still letting the Leinenkugels do my talking for me. "Forgive me for asking, Garth, but what does that have to do with anything?"

I answered his question with a question. "If Amel Pilkin wasn't murdered, then why is someone trying so hard to erase all trace of him?"

"How do you know someone is trying to erase all traces?" Clarkie asked.

"Outside of the fire?" Even Clarkie couldn't ignore that.

"Yes, outside of the fire."

"I'll let you know once I look inside that van."

Hidden Quarry was about two miles south of Oakalla back a narrow, deeply rutted dirt road, overgrown with trees and brush that scraped the side of the patrol car as we drove through. So named because you could drive right up to it, even into it, before you saw the danger, Hidden Quarry had been abandoned years ago, and the thick woods surrounding it now grew to its edge. But it had remained an attraction for swimmers, hunters, fishermen, and lovers, who found its near-perfect isolation ideal for their purposes. Luckily for Clarkie and me, the dirt road was frozen solid, or we never could have traveled it.

Clarkie took his flashlight out of the patrol car and shined it down into the quarry. I could see the van resting at the edge of the rock and just beyond it, the deep green waters of the quarry that seemed to take forever to freeze, even in the coldest winters.

"Clarkie, shut off your light a minute," I said.

Without the light, I had a quarter moon and a sky full of stars to see by. Out here, as at grandmother's farm, the stars seemed nearer and brighter than in town.

"I think I'll chance it without the light," I said. "I'll need both hands to hold on."

"I don't know, Garth," Clarkie said while looking over the rim of the quarry. "It's a long way down there. I'm not sure you ought to risk it."

"What other choice do we have?"

"We could always call the University of Wisconsin and let them worry about it."

"Not yet, Clarkie. Maybe later."

As a kid, I had spent several weeks each summer visiting Grandmother Ryland. I had been up and down the quarry wall many times while wearing nothing more than a smile. I had dived into its icy-cold waters, swum like hell to keep from cramping, and then climbed out to lie on a shelf of rock in the hot sun while the other kids took their turn. Sometimes, particularly on a night like this as I groped for every foothold and clung to every rock like a monkey to its mother, I wondered what had happened to that kid. I hoped he had gotten smarter as he had gotten older, instead of just losing his nerve.

Finally I reached the van, which was even closer to the edge than I first thought and so precariously balanced that I was afraid to even approach it for fear of sending it over the edge.

"What's the problem, Garth?" Clarkie said, shining his light into my eyes.

I told him what the problem was.

"Can I help in any way?"

"Pray for me, Clarkie," I said as I approached the van. "And shut that damn light off."

Then I discovered another problem. While the windows of the van were both rolled about a quarter of the way down, presumably to help it sink once it hit the water, its doors were locked. To unlock either one of them, I had either to stand on my tiptoes with my arm inside the van, feeling for a lock I couldn't see, or to break a window with a rock and run the risk of sending the van into the water. I broke out a window with a rock. Better it than me.

The van teetered from the blow but stayed on the edge of the rock. I reached inside the broken window, found the door lock, and carefully tripped it. Then I opened the door. The van teetered again, rocking several inches back and forth before slowly coming to a rest. Any weight at all on it would likely send it over the edge, but I had to see inside it, and its dome light wasn't working.

"Clarkie, throw me the flashlight," I said, wishing now that I'd brought it with me. When canoeing Sugar Creek back in Indiana, I once had someone throw me a can of pop off a high bridge. I caught it, but it nearly knocked me out of the canoe, and my hands stung for days afterwards.

But this time I got off easy. Clarkie threw the flashlight over my head and into the quarry. I forgot that Clarkie took things literally. I should have told him to drop the flashlight.

"So much for that idea," I said.

"What's that, Garth?"

"Nothing, Clarkie. Do you have any rope in your car?"

"No."

"How about a chain?"

"Not that I know of."

"Forget it then." I would have asked him to cut me a grapevine, but I doubted that he had a hatchet in his car, either.

To get where I wanted to go, which was into the back of the van, I had to go all the way inside and then climb between the seats. I knew I couldn't make it without sending the van into the water. But I hoped I could get out before the van went all the way under.

It worked out the way I expected it to. The instant I climbed inside the van, it began to slide into the water. I scrambled between the seats and into the back where I found Amel Pilkin wrapped in a sheet. As cold as it was outside, Amel should have been frozen hard as a rock. But he wasn't. The van had been sitting on the north wall of the quarry, facing the sun. So when I grabbed him to carry him out of there, Amel hissed at me. The smell nearly knocked me out.

Then the water rushed in upon me, bowling me over and causing me to lose my hold on Amel. Claustrophobic, I hated all closed-in places, and my worst nightmare was to be trapped inside something with no way out. I panicked. I no longer cared about saving Amel. All I cared about was saving myself.

Grabbing the seats, I forced my way to the front of the van. But the door I'd gone in had been squeezed closed by the pressure of the water upon it. Pushing against it until I thought I'd burst, I still couldn't force it open. That meant I had to go out the broken window.

I felt for the window and found it, stuck my nose to the top of the van for one last breath of air, swam out into the quarry, and surfaced a few feet away. I'd experienced hypothermia before and nearly died from it. I didn't have to be told to get out of the water posthaste.

Once I reached shore, I lay on the rock a moment before I began the long climb back up to the top. Clarkie was shouting something at me, but I didn't answer. There he was, still at the top. There I was at the bottom, far out of his reach. I was glad my life hadn't depended on him.

We rode in silence back to Oakalla. Though the fan and the heat were both turned on high, I shivered and shook the whole way. From fear perhaps as much as the cold. Fear of what might have happened, even though it hadn't happened.

"I'm sorry, Garth." Clarkie finally broke the silence as we pulled up in front of my house. "I saw the van going under, but I didn't know how to stop it. So like a big dummy, I just stood there."

"It's okay," I said. "There wasn't much you could do anyway."

"At least I could have tried."

"Forget it, Clarkie. I'm too cold to argue."

I went into the house where Ruth sat reading in the living room and a fire burned in the fireplace. I removed the screen, stripped down to my boxer shorts, and crouched beside the fire. Maybe I'd be warm by summer, but I doubted it.

Ruth got up and went into the kitchen. A few minutes

later she returned. "Here, drink this," she said, handing me what smelled like a hot toddy.

"Are you sure it'll help?" I said, hating to move my arm even six inches away from the fire to take the glass from her.

"I'm sure."

Ruth was right. The hot toddy helped. And after I'd put on my robe that she brought me, I began to feel almost warm. But I still kept close to the fire.

"Do you want to tell me what happened?" Ruth said.

"If you promise not to laugh."

Laughter, however, seemed to be the last thing on Ruth's mind when I finished. "Garth, whatever possessed you?" she said. "Just what were you trying to prove anyway?"

"I wasn't trying to prove anything," I said. I turned to warm my backside. "I was trying to get Amel out of the van."

"For what purpose? He's been dead a week now. You weren't saving him from anything."

"Except a water grave."

"Think about it, Garth," she said sternly. "How is that any worse than being cut on by a bunch of medical students? If I had my choice in the matter, I'd rather be at the bottom of Hidden Quarry."

"It wasn't your choice. It was Amel's."

"So you risked life and limb to give it to him. Garth, that would be a poor risk even if he were alive. Dead, it borders on lunacy."

"I'm not crazy, Ruth," I said, trying to convince the both of us. "Maybe what I did was crazy, and I'm not sure I'd ever do it again, but even at that, I had a reason. If somebody took the trouble to steal a van from the University of Wisconsin, then used it to steal Amel's body in an attempt to send him to the bottom of Hidden Quarry, then whoever did it knows something about Amel's death that we don't. My guess is that he knows Amel was murdered and was trying to get rid of the evidence."

She didn't say anything.

"Or doesn't that make sense to **you?**"

"Yes, that makes sense to me," she said. "But what you did doesn't make sense to me. You could have accomplished the same thing a whole lot easier with Danny Palmer's wrecker cable attached to the van. And done it in the daylight as well."

She was right. But I wouldn't admit it. "What's your point?"

"My point is that you wanted to be a hero all by yourself. And you nearly got yourself killed in the bargain. That's my point," she repeated in case I missed it the first time.

"So I made a mistake," I said. "I've made them before."

"Not the size of this one," she insisted. "You've never tried to rescue a dead man before."

I thought long and hard, but I couldn't come up with an answer for her. So I did the next best thing. I went to bed.

15

AT DAYBREAK THE next morning I called Ben Bryan, the county coroner, and told him what I wished he would do. Next I called Clarkie and found him at home.

"Clarkie, this is Garth. I have a favor to ask."

"Name it," he said eagerly. "After last night, I feel I owe you one."

"I'm looking for the owner of a late-model grey Mercedes convertible who lives in the Madison area. See how many there are and who owns them. Also, if you would, Clarkie, keep what happened last night under your hat, and that includes the Banner brothers, if they haven't told anyone yet. I'd just as soon that not everyone in Oakalla know about that van."

"What was in it?" he said. "I was so shook up after you went in the water, I forgot to ask."

"Amel Pilkin."

Clarkie didn't take the news well. "The same Amel Pilkin who Orville Goodnight found dead last Saturday morning?"

"The very same."

"I thought he'd be in Madison by now."

"So did I, Clarkie. So did a lot of other people."

"So you're still at it," Ruth said the instant I hung up. If I were to judge by the sound of her voice, she didn't approve.

"Still at it," I said. I had hoped to be gone before she ever got up.

She went to the stove, took out the coffeepot, and filled it with tap water. "I thought you would be. Last night didn't teach you a thing, did it?"

"It taught me not to go swimming in the middle of November again."

She didn't say anything. She often didn't say anything when she thought I was being stupid.

"What do you want from me, Ruth? I thought we agreed that I couldn't quit on this thing, even if I wanted to."

She rummaged through the cupboards on the pretense of looking for the coffee. But she knew where it was all along. "That was before last night," she said.

"I told you it wouldn't happen again."

"That's not the point," she said. But she wouldn't say anything more.

The phone rang. It was Ben Bryan. "I called the head of the medical school there in Madison," he said, "and asked him why they didn't pick up Amel Pilkin last Monday like they planned. You know what he said? He said somebody called from here to tell them that we needed to keep Amel's body awhile longer and that we'd let them know when we were through with it."

"Thanks, Ben. I thought that might have happened."

"But why? Does that make any sense to you, Garth, to go to all the trouble to steal a body?"

"It's starting to. I'll let you know how much sense when I learn more."

"Well?" Ruth said after I'd hung up.

"I thought you weren't interested."

"I never said I wasn't interested. I just said that it wasn't in your best interest to be."

"Same difference, it seems to me."

"Not by a long shot, Garth. Not from where I stand."

So I told her what Ben Bryan had told me.

She thought it over, then said, "So whoever planned to steal Amel's body and dump it in Hidden Quarry had to have had outside help. Otherwise, Ben Bryan would have recognized him."

"That's my thinking. Yes."

"And you believe the man who owns the grey Mercedes convertible that you saw in Claire Huffer's lane is the outside help?"

"Yes. That's what I believe. Or if he's not the outside help, then he's the one who hired it."

"That doesn't speak too well for Claire Huffer," she said.

"Or Whitey Huffer," I was just as quick to point out.

An hour later I got into Jessie and left for Madison. Clarkie had come up with the names of five people in the Madison area who owned late-model grey Mercedes convertibles. I planned to talk to all of them if I could, or as many as I thought I needed to. But first I planned to visit the bank where Whitey Huffer, up until the day he became sheriff, had worked as a security guard.

It was an old established bank on Broadway near the heart of downtown Madison. I parked Jessie in the bank's parking lot and went inside where I took a seat and looked things over. The outside of the bank had a black marble cornice supported by white marble pillars, and its name, First Fidelity Union, printed in gold letters on the door. Inside, it had a black marble floor, heavy oak doors to all of the offices, oak wainscoting, and a white marble wall beneath the teller cages. The feel of the bank was cool, crisp, and clean, like a freshly minted greenback.

"Are you waiting for someone?"

I looked up to see a pretty young woman in a blue-and-white polka-dot dress smiling at me. She wore bright red lipstick and high heels, and her brown hair was long and curled. She also wore either nylons or panty hose, but I didn't ask her which.

"Actually I'm looking for Whitey Huffer," I said. "But I don't see him anywhere around."

I watched her closely for her reaction and got more than

I bargained for. Her smile vanished as tears came into her eyes. She had to take a moment to compose herself.

"Mr. Huffer doesn't work here anymore," she said in her best professional voice. "He quit without notice a couple weeks ago."

"Do you have any idea where he went?"

She had more than an idea. "I heard he got elected sheriff or something back in that small town where he lives," she said. "But it can't be much of a job, if they expect Whitey Huffer to do it."

"Is that experience talking?"

"That's Ginger Wright talking. If and when you see Whitey Huffer, you can tell him that for me."

"Miss Wright," I heard a man's deep voice from behind me say, "I believe you have customers waiting."

The change in her was instantaneous. She went from being in charge to being in trouble. With a look of chagrin, she returned to her receptionist desk, like a schoolgirl who had just been chided by her teacher.

I turned to see who had spoken to her. He was a large bald man with bulbous eyes and thick jowls and wearing a three-piece grey suit, a dark red tie, and burgundy wingtip shoes. I guessed he was somewhere in his late fifties or early sixties.

"How do you know I'm not a customer?" I said.

"I make it my business to know."

"And you are?"

"Lincoln Thomas, president of First Fidelity Union." He said it as if I already should know who he was.

"Glad to meet you, Mr. Thomas."

I didn't offer to shake his hand. He didn't offer to shake mine.

"And you are?" he said.

"Garth Ryland. I'm a friend of Whitey Huffer's."

"From where?"

"Around," I said.

"What is your business with Whitey Huffer?"

"I'm afraid that's personal, Mr. Thomas."

"Follow me."

He crooked his fat forefinger and turned toward the outside door. As he did, I saw the security guard across the lobby from us take a couple steps our way. I thought that I was about to be booted out of the bank when Lincoln Thomas opened the oak door nearest the entrance and started up a wooden staircase. I followed him up it and into his office where he sat down at an oak desk that was nearly as large as mine. But I bet that his hadn't come from his father's dairy.

"Have a seat," he said.

I sat down in a straight-backed oak chair facing him, hoping he'd make the first move. But he just sat there staring at me through half-opened eyes, like a big drowsy cat at a small mouse. Sunlight streamed in through his office window and onto his desk. It was warm, almost mellow in there. I yawned.

"Have you ever played poker, Mr. Ryland?" he finally asked.

"A time or two. Why?"

"I thought so. You have a poker face. You're very hard to read."

"Likewise, I'm sure."

"So let's cut the crap and get down to business," he said, ignoring my last comment. "What do you want with Whitey Huffer?"

"Why do you want to know?"

His eyes narrowed a little and hardened. He was used to asking the questions, not answering them. Giving the orders, not taking them.

"Let's just say that as his former employer, I have a vested interest in Whitey Huffer," he said.

"Let's just say that I have a vested interest in Whitey Huffer, too."

He reached into his top desk drawer and took out what

appeared to be a checkbook. "How much does he owe you?" he said.

"Ten thousand dollars, give or take a couple hundred." I figured that would at least get his attention.

He wrote furiously for a few seconds then handed me a check for ten thousand dollars. "Now let me have the markers," he said.

I had to think fast. That was almost too much to ask on a sleepy Saturday morning. "I can't. They're at home. I didn't expect to get the money today."

He took the check back before I could pocket it. "When I get the markers, you get the check," he said. "Not before."

I had what I'd come for. It was time to hit the road.

But Lincoln Thomas was a step ahead of me. "If not the money, what did you expect to get today?" he said before I could make good my escape.

I sat back down in my chair. I didn't want to appear too eager to go, even though my shoes were already starting to smoke. "Excuses," I said. "That's what I expected to get today." Then since I didn't know what else to say, I added, "You know Whitey."

"Yes," he said bitterly. "I know Whitey."

"Now I have a question for you," I said, deciding to push my luck. "Why bail him out? He made his bed. Why not let him sleep in it?"

His eyes narrowed to slits. I didn't like the look in them. "That, my friend, is between Whitey Huffer and me. You have your money, or will have when I get the markers. So why don't you leave while you're still ahead."

I didn't have to be told twice. But on my way out, I stopped at Ginger Wright's desk. "Thanks, Ginger," I said. "I hope I didn't get you into any trouble with your boss."

She looked around for Lincoln Thomas before she said, "It's not you who got me in trouble. Whitey Huffer's been nothing but trouble for me ever since I've known him."

"Too bad about his gambling," I said.

"Too bad about a lot of things," she answered, and the tears reappeared in her eyes.

Her phone rang at the same time that I saw the security guard reach for his beeper. I thought I knew who was calling both of them.

"Yes, Mr. Thomas," I heard her say. "He's on his way out the door now."

16

BYRON WINTERS WAS the first person on Clarkie's list of those in Madison who owned late-model grey Mercedes convertibles. Byron Winters was a surgeon in his early fifties who lived on Lake Mendota and whose office was in the clinic attached to University Hospital. I didn't know if surgeons kept Saturday morning office hours or not, but I went to the clinic and found out that Byron Winters did.

His receptionist gave me a form to fill out while I waited to see if there would be any openings that morning. Otherwise, I would have to come back on Monday. So I filled out the form, listed vasectomy as my reason for wanting surgery, and put Doc Airhart down as my family physician. Then I picked out a couple copies of *Sports Illustrated*, settled back in my padded wooden chair, and prepared myself for a long wait. I didn't mind, since the room was warm and sunlit, and I was the only one in there.

A woman came out of the door to the right of the receptionist, stopped a moment at the receptionist's desk, and left. A moment later a man wearing black shoes, black slacks, a light-blue, button-down, long-sleeved shirt, and a dark blue tie appeared at the door that the woman had just come out of.

"Mr. Ryland?" he said.

I held up my hand. "That's me."

I stood and stretched, then followed him into an examining room in the back of the building. He was of medium height with a slender build, short grey hair, square shoulders, and a stiff military walk and bearing. On first impression, I would have guessed that he had been a military doctor at one time.

"So, Doc Airhart referred you to me," he said after closing the door of the examining room. "I didn't know that old scoundrel was still seeing patients."

"He doesn't usually. I'm a special case."

He put on some disposable gloves. "Drop your pants," he said. "Let's get on with this."

"You can't have a golf match waiting," I said, wondering what I'd gotten myself into.

"No, a tennis match," he said.

"In this weather?"

"Indoors. Your pants."

I undid my belt and dropped my pants. I'd gone this far. I might as well see it all the way through.

Byron Winters was a thorough, though not a gentle man. By the time he finished his examination, I felt as I had the day of my draft physical, that if there was anything worth finding, he would have found it.

"You can put your pants back on," he said. He took off his gloves and threw them away.

I put my pants back on.

He was looking at the form I'd filled out. "I see here that you're not married," he said.

"I was married," I said. "Now I'm divorced." For over eleven years now, though it didn't seem that long.

"Any children?"

"One. He died on his first birthday."

He made a note of that. "Do you think you might want to have any children in the future?" he asked.

"It's getting kind of late, isn't it?"

He shrugged. "It depends on what you want to call late. Men in their sixties, even in their seventies and eighties, can father children. It depends on how badly you want to leave a legacy."

"Not that badly," I said. Which wasn't exactly true but true enough.

"You're sure?" His blue eyes were cold, clear, and deep, like several northern lakes I knew.

"I'm sure."

"Then I'll put you down for ten a.m. two weeks from today. We can do it on an outpatient basis here at the hospital."

"I'll be there," I said, not believing a word of it.

I stopped at the door of the examining room on my way out. I had yet to ask him what I'd come for, but I no longer felt the need. Byron Winters was exactly what he seemed to be, which was a cool competent surgeon who liked to play tennis.

"Was there something else?" he said.

"You wouldn't happen to know a Whitey Huffer, would you?"

"No. Not that I recall. Why do you ask?" The name apparently meant nothing to him.

"No reason," I said and left.

Randolph Cunningham III was playing football with his son along the west shore of Lake Mendota. A stockbroker in his mid-thirties, Randolph Cunningham III had his grey Mercedes convertible parked in his drive when I arrived at his house. It could have been the one I'd seen in Claire Huffer's drive.

Randolph Cunningham III and his son, who I guessed to be no more than twelve, both wore Nike tennis shoes, sweat pants, headbands, and red University of Wisconsin football jerseys. Both were tall, lean, and blond, and both had strong right arms for throwing the football and good hands for catching it, though of the two of them, the boy was actually the better receiver. His cuts were smoother and sharper than his dad's, and he was willing to lay out to catch the ball, whereas his dad wasn't.

I watched them for several minutes from the knoll above them, envying them the whole time. Had things turned out differently, they could have been my son and me.

"Is there something I can help you with?" Randolph Cunningham III asked me on his way back up to his house.

His son ran on ahead of us and threw a pass to himself.

"I hear you're a stockbroker." I offered my hand. "I'm in the market for one."

"Do you live in the neighborhood?" He shook my hand.

"No, a friend of mine referred me to you. Whitey Huffer. He spoke highly of you."

Cunningham looked puzzled. "I don't know a Whitey Huffer."

"He's a friend of a friend."

"Who is?"

"Lincoln Thomas."

Cunningham frowned. "The banker? I don't know him either except by reputation."

"He seems to know you," I said.

His frown deepened. "I don't know how," he said then left it at that.

We turned to watch his son who just had made a diving fingertip catch of a long pass. He spiked the ball. Touchdown.

"You ever play the game?" Randolph Cunningham III asked.

"Only for fun."

He smiled. He seemed to know what I meant. When adults stepped in and started running things, games stopped being fun.

"I used to play quarterback in high school," he said. "Then I was a backup quarterback here at Wisconsin. Usually third or fourth string. I think I got in two games in three years." He watched his son with admiring eyes. "But it's a great game, right?"

"Right," I agreed. And meant it. "And I bet you have tickets to the game this afternoon."

"As a matter of fact, we do," he said. "We were just on our way in to clean up."

"I won't keep you then. Maybe we can talk business another day."

"Wait," he said. "Let me get you one of my cards."

He ran toward the house, caught a pass from his son on the way, and flipped the football behind his back, back to his son. I wondered if his son, too, would star in high school and then end up on the taxi squad at the University of Wisconsin; or if he would go on to bigger and better things; or if he would even play football at all once he left home, or even once he left the eighth grade. Whatever he decided to do with his life, I wished him well.

Randolph Cunningham III returned with his business card. "I'm sorry you made the drive all the way here for nothing," he said.

"It wasn't for nothing," I said. And left.

Rory O'Conner was, in no particular order, an Irishman, lawyer, former state senator, and former congressman, who owned the Fisherman's restaurant that overlooked the east shore of Lake Monona. I'd eaten at the Fisherman's on several occasions. Except for those you caught, cleaned, and cooked, then ate right there on shore as the waves lapped at your feet, it served the best wall-eyed pike around.

I'd missed the noon rush hours, so by the time I got to the Fisherman's, I had it almost to myself. The hostess seated me next to a window where I could look out over the lake. I ordered a fish sandwich and a draft of Leinenkugels.

Unlike Lake Mendota, which still had open water and flocks of ducks and geese upon it, Lake Monona was iced over. Clear and smooth, it dazzled where the sun's rays hit its hard surface and shattered into a million tiny shards of white light. But in the shadows, which had already claimed its west shore, it looked cold and forbidding, and more like night than day.

The waitress brought my fish sandwich and Leinenkugels. I bit into the sandwich and burned my mouth. But it was worth it.

"Can I get you anything else?" the waitress asked when I'd finished. Already they were setting up more tables, getting ready for the crowd that would fill the place and keep it filled once the football game was over.

"I'd like to talk to Mr. O'Conner if he's around."

In the past Rory O'Conner and I had talked on several occasions. He liked to talk to his customers, and they liked to talk to him.

She made a face that might have meant anything. "He's around. But I'm not sure that he'll talk to you."

She left the room. Moments later a tall, well-dressed, solemn woman came to my table. She wore lots of jewelry, lots of makeup, and bags under her eyes. Like Ruth, she appeared to be in her early seventies and had class as well as dignity. Unlike Ruth, she had strength without vigor. Hers seemed the strength of money and position, borrowed rather than earned in the school of hard knocks.

"Janet said you wanted to see Mr. O'Conner," she said.

"If he's available." I was starting to believe that he wasn't.

"May I ask why?" She had carefully noted my jeans and flannel shirt and rightfully determined that I probably wasn't on her Christmas card list.

"I'm an old fan of his. We used to talk politics whenever I would come in here to eat."

"And how long ago was that?"

I counted the years and realized that it had been longer than I'd thought. "Maybe three years ago." The last time I had been in there was with Diana, and she had been out of my life for over two years now.

"That explains it then," she said. "Mr. O'Conner hasn't been well for the past two years. He hasn't been up to visitors for at least the past year."

"I'm sorry. I didn't know that."

"Not everyone does. Just those who come here regularly."

Though she spoke graciously, I felt the barb beneath her words. Had I been a better customer, I would have known the situation.

"I suppose then that he doesn't get the chance to drive much anymore," I said.

She looked at me in horror as if I'd lost my mind. "He doesn't get the chance to drive at all. How could he? He can't even feed himself."

I looked out at Lake Monona where the shadows had grown ever longer and now ruled half the lake. "That's too bad," I said. "I know how well he liked that Mercedes of his."

She gave me a strange look. But then this was a strange conversation. "You're confused," she said. "I'm the one who owns the Mercedes. Mr. O'Conner has never owned a foreign car in his life. He wouldn't have one, he said, if they gave it to him."

I smiled. "That sounds like him," I said.

She didn't return my smile. "Yes, it does, doesn't it," she said. "Just like him."

Once outside I looked at the list Clarkie had given me to see if the mistake had been mine or his. There it was, the car was registered to Fisherman's. I had just assumed it was Rory O'Conner's car.

Max Dieter owned Madison Instruments, an electronics factory on the east side of Madison. When I had called his home to see if he was there, his wife said I would find him at the factory. From the tone of her voice, I guessed that it was presumptuous to expect to find him anywhere else.

Max Dieter was a big bandy-legged, barrel-chested man with a wide face, rosy cheeks, and thick grey hair, who spoke with a heavy German accent. I had found him in his office after I had let myself in the front door. His grey Mercedes convertible was the only car in the parking lot. He appeared to be alone in the factory.

"So," he said to me, "you want to do a story on Madison Instruments."

"No," I said. "I want to do a story on Max Dieter."

"Why do you want to do a story on me?" he asked. "What have I done to deserve one?" He hadn't embraced the idea of a story on him and his factory as heartily as I thought he would. Actually, he hadn't embraced it at all.

"You're an obvious success," I said, winging it as I went along. "And people like to read about success."

"Yes," he said, still cautious. "But why me, Max Dieter? There are hundreds of other people around who are a success. Am I not right?"

He sat back in his office chair with his feet upon his desk. He had his white shirt sleeves rolled up to his elbows and his tie loosened at the collar. Though he didn't appear to be on edge, he didn't appear to be relaxed either.

"True," I said. Then I took a chance and said, "But how many of them are first generation Americans?"

"And how many of them learned to speak English by taking German at the college?" For the first time since I'd been there, he seemed to let his guard down.

"Exactly," I said. "You're a self-made man. What most of us would like to be and aren't."

He shook his head vigorously, as he took his feet from the desk and sat up in his chair. "No, no, that's not true. No one is a self-made man. If he says that, then he is, by God, a liar!" He slammed his fist down on the desk.

"Then you've had help along the way?"

He rose from his desk and stood at the window, looking through the slits in his venetian blind at the street outside. "Yes. I have had help," he said, his accent thickening. "Lots of help."

I waited for him to continue. When he didn't continue, I said, "Who gave you the most help? Was it someone in your family or someone on the outside?"

He didn't answer.

"Mr. Dieter?"

He turned to face me. He looked sad and weary. "I think, Mr. Ryland, that I have answered enough questions for one day. Perhaps if you choose to come back one day in the future, we might talk."

"How far in the future?" The newspaperman in me had taken over. I smelled a real story here that might have nothing to do with Whitey Huffer.

"I don't know," he said. "If you will leave your card, perhaps I will call you. Perhaps not."

I took out one of my business cards and laid it on his desk. "How do you like your new Mercedes?" I asked. "A friend of mine, Whitey Huffer, swears by his."

Though he was looking right at me, he didn't seem to be seeing me. Neither had the name Whitey Huffer seemed to register.

"I beg your pardon."

"Your new Mercedes, the one parked outside. How do you like it?"

"I like it fine," he said without enthusiasm.

"It is possibly the best engineered car in the world." He walked to his desk, set aside my card, and shuffled through some papers. "I should know about that. I am also an engineer."

"So is my father," I said, as if that explained anything.

He continued to shuffle papers. "Good. That is good."

I thought that was the end of our conversation. But his next statement stopped me at his office door.

"Some of us are proud to be German, you know."

I turned to face him. He didn't appear to be making a statement, but stating a fact. "I know," I said.

He nodded solemnly and turned his attention to the papers on the desk.

I went outside and got into Jessie. Taking Clarkie's list of names from my shirt pocket, I looked at the remaining name on the list. Then I looked at the shadows that had covered everything but the roof of Madison Instruments. Maybe another day.

17

RUTH AND I sat at the kitchen table. At six p.m. it was already dark outside; at seven p.m. she planned to be on her way to bowl with her team. I had already told her about my day. She had already told me about hers. Neither one of us had said much after that.

"So what do you plan to do now?" she asked.

Ruth wore black slacks, white tennis shoes, and her league bowling shirt, which was purple trimmed in gold. I had tried to get her to buy purple slacks to match her shirt, but she had balked at that idea. She said that a purple shirt was bad enough. With matching purple slacks, she might as well pin a red light bulb on her.

"Now I wait," I said. "The next move is Whitey Huffer's."

"What makes you so sure he'll do anything?"

"I don't know that he will, Ruth. It depends on whether I touched a raw nerve today."

"Do you think you did?"

I shrugged. "Only time will tell."

Ruth rose to fill a glass with ice water. She never drank coffee before she bowled because she said it made her too nervous. The one time she had drunk coffee before a match, which was years ago, she had thrown one of her balls so hard that it had broken the pinspotter. She said she was lucky that there wasn't a ball boy back there, or she might have killed him.

"Tell me again what your thinking is," she said as she returned to the table.

"My thinking is that Whitey Huffer is deep in debt over his gambling losses and that is why Claire Huffer is selling the land to Bench-Mart, in order to pay them off. And I think the real reason he ran for sheriff, and why she campaigned so hard for him, was to get him away from Madison and his debts."

"So why not let it go at that?" she said.

"I would, if he hadn't killed Amel Pilkin."

"You don't know that's the case."

"No. But it's a good guess," I said. "You remember there in the Corner Bar and Grill last Friday when Amel waved an envelope at me, then started hugging himself. I think that whatever it was he had, he'd found it in Whitey Huffer's trash. Or maybe even in Carolyn Fleischower's trash, since Whitey has been known to spend time there."

Ruth took one drink of her ice water and set it aside. She really didn't like to drink ice water in winter. She was just killing time until her ride arrived.

"Such as?" she said. "What could possibly be in Whitey's trash that would be worth killing Amel over?"

"That's what I don't know," I said. "But Amel was surely excited about something. Maybe he found one of Whitey's old gambling markers."

"You mean one he'd paid off and thrown away?" Ruth's face said she was skeptical. "Why would Amel get so excited over that? He probably wouldn't even know what he had."

"Maybe not at first. But then he might have realized something was up when he saw Whitey come into the Corner Bar and Grill after him."

For something to do, she walked to the sink, dumped her ice water out, and returned to her seat again. It was like this every night she bowled. She even made me nervous.

"I don't know, Garth," she said. "Your theory has a lot of holes in it. For one thing, Amel was already excited about something long before Whitey Huffer ever walked into the Corner Bar and Grill. For another, if he did have something on Whitey Huffer, why would Amel bother telling you about it?"

"Amel liked me," I said. "And he knew how much I didn't like Whitey Huffer."

"So you think Whitey followed Amel when he left the Corner Bar and Grill last Friday night. And did what? Pulled him over, hit him on the head, and left him in his truck to die?"

"Something like that."

"I don't buy it, Garth. That sounds pretty hardhearted, even for Whitey Huffer."

"Then explain to me how Amel got that knot on the back of his head."

She went to the front door to see if her ride was there yet. Then she returned to the kitchen where she stood looking out the south window. She knew Wanda Collum would be late, since Wanda Collum was always late. But that still didn't keep her from watching at the window.

"I can't explain to you how Amel got that knot on his head," she said. "Or where the trash went that you think was in his truck. Or for that matter who burned his place down, if that's what happened to it. But you still have nothing to go on, except your own feelings for Whitey Huffer."

That angered me. "So you're saying that this is a witch hunt on my part?"

"I'm saying for you to keep your eyes and your mind open. That's all."

She saw her ride coming. I could tell by the way her eyes lit up. She picked up her coat and purse on her way out of the kitchen. The front door opened and closed, and whoosh, she was gone.

I sat in the suddenly silent kitchen, wondering what I should do with the rest of my Saturday night. I could always build a fire and sit by it with a tall stiff highball for company. Or if I wanted real company, I could always go up to the Corner Bar and Grill. Or I could always go to my office, fix myself a cup of instant coffee, and pretend to work.

The phone rang. I thought it might be Whitey Huffer. I turned out to be right.

"Ryland, this is your last warning," he said. "Stay out of my life or pay the price."

"Which is what?"

"You figure it out."

"It might be a lot easier on all of us, Whitey, if you'd just come clean. You might lose your job, but that would probably be the worst that would happen. That is, if you didn't kill Amel Pilkin."

"I didn't kill anybody, God damn it. How many times do I have to tell you that?" He slurred his words as if he'd been drinking.

"Then you've got nothing to worry about."

"Says you," he said.

"I'm listening."

He hesitated as if he were thinking it over. Then he said, "You had your warning, Ryland. Make the most of it." He hung up.

I stood there with the receiver in my hand for a long time before I put it back on the cradle. I thought about calling Claire Huffer and asking her to try to talk some sense into Whitey, but in the end decided against it. If she were somehow involved, and I couldn't quite convince myself that she wasn't, I didn't want to know about it until I had to.

18

I LEFT THE house a half hour later, wearing dark-blue tennis shoes, black socks, dark-blue jeans, a black turtleneck, dark-brown cotton gloves, and a black stocking cap pulled all the way down to my navel. Even at that, I shivered. From the excitement, I thought, rather than the cold.

Then Jessie didn't want to start. Like the Sunday before at Carolyn Fleischower's, she ground for several seconds before she fired, then sputtered for several more seconds before she decided to go. The first chance I had, I planned to take her to Danny Palmer to see what was wrong this time. With any luck, it would be terminal.

I drove to Pilkin's Knob, parked Jessie next to the blackened remains of Amel Pilkin's house, and started across country toward Claire Huffer's farm. I remembered Claire telling me that they got rid of their big things in the dump out back. Where "out back" was, I didn't know. Somewhere within two thousand acres, which was roughly three square miles.

But I guessed that for convenience sake, the dump would be fairly close to the house, since most dumps were continuations of old dumps started generations before. The dump turned out to be located in a deep ravine within two hundred yards of the house, which was closer to the house than I wanted to be.

I stood for a moment in the moonlight, listening to the

night sounds, and the farm sounds, and the sound of my heart pounding in my chest. Then I yawned, the way I used to before every basketball game, track meet, or baseball game, or any other contest where something was clearly at stake. Then I went down into the ravine.

My plan was not to use the flashlight I carried until it was absolutely necessary. The moonlight was bright enough for me to see shapes and outlines, and if I needed to see something in more detail, I would turn the flashlight on then. Otherwise, it might be seen from the house.

Rummaging through old dumps had long been a fascination of mine. I delighted in the century-old whiskey bottle that I had found in a gold miner's dump in Colorado and in the turn-of-the-century medicine bottles that I found on my aunt's sandhill farm in Indiana. And the shelves in my office at the *Oakalla Reporter* were lined with treasures that I'd found in the other dumps.

I also had a short deep scar on my hand and a long wide scar on my knee that I'd gotten in dumps. That was the trouble with dumps. To get to the best stuff, you had to get to the very bottom of them. To get to the very bottom of them, you had to dig your way through glass, metal, earth, and rust. Unless you were careful how you dug and where you put your feet, you were asking for trouble.

Once I reached the very bottom of the ravine, I stopped to rest. I felt as if I'd been walking on eggs the whole way and my clothes were soaked with sweat. So far I'd found four fairly new fifty-five gallon drums that could have belonged to Amel Pilkin, since they were what he usually carried in the back of his pickup to hold the trash; and several newly deposited cans and bottles that could have come from the drums. But I'd found nothing that told me why Amel Pilkin had died.

Then I saw something smooth and shiny glint in the moonlight. I bent down to examine it and discovered a toaster oven that looked like new. When I first shined the flashlight inside it, I thought that someone had taped a cigarette to the top of it. But the cigarette turned out to be a small vial of white powder.

I took the vial out of the toaster oven and tasted the powder. It tasted bitter to me. But I didn't think it was alum. I taped the vial back in place and took the toaster oven along as I continued my search.

Three times I used my flashlight. The first time was when I'd found the toaster oven. The second time was when I'd lost my tennis shoe in a snarl of wire and had to find it again. The third time I used my flashlight, I used it to identify the sport coat that along with several others I'd found rolled up and stuck in the hopper of an old planter. It was the same red plaid sport coat that Amel Pilkin was wearing the last time I saw him alive.

I tried to carry the sport coat in one hand and the toaster oven in the other, but I had no balance that way and no way to carry my flashlight. So I put the sport coat on over my windbreaker and the flashlight in the sport coat's inside pocket. I felt about ten pounds heavier but less awkward than before.

While I stopped to remove a tin can from my shoe, I heard a twig snap on the ridge above me. I set the toaster oven on the ground and crouched down as far as I could get. Apparently I didn't act fast enough. Someone shot a hole in the toaster oven.

I didn't wait for the second shot to hit me. I picked up the toaster oven and took off down the ravine as fast as I could go. The second shot hit right beside me and sent something sharp into my ankle. But I didn't stop to see what.

I soon put the dump behind me and just as soon discovered that I could run faster but no easier than before. The ravine had its own obstacles in the form of bushes, briers, and low-hanging tree limbs. Every time I ran into one, it seemed I left another little part of me behind. Not just my flesh hurt either. My arms, legs, lungs, and heart all cried out for rest. I felt that if I didn't stop to rest soon, I would run myself to death.

So at the next thicket I stopped. Since I was headed north, the ravine had to end sometime before I got to Lake Superior. Either that or it was going to be a long night. While I rested, I looked and listened for my pursuer who had shot at me two more times as I ran down the ravine. Seeing no one, I took off again. The instant after I did, a slug tore through the bush where I'd been standing.

The toaster oven, I thought. Get rid of the toaster oven, and then whoever is shooting at you won't be able to see you. I liked that idea. It made sense to me.

What I didn't like was the prospect of going back there and finding it missing and of giving up the slim chance of finding out whoever it was who owned it. I didn't know what the vial of white powder was, but I had a pretty good idea. However, it didn't come with a serial number. The toaster oven, on the other hand, did.

The ravine began to narrow and climb. I started uphill, slipped, and came down hard on the toaster oven, knocking the wind out of me. I left the toaster oven lying there on the ground. Whatever good it might do me, it wasn't worth my life.

The ravine ended on high ground. From there I made good progress until I came to a fence and ran out of cover at the same time. The fence proved no problem. I went up and over it easily. But the frozen plowed field on the other side of the fence took my legs out from under me before I had taken five steps. Then I had to get up and run in moonlight all the way across it.

Once, I'd jumped a rabbit in a picked bean field and shot at him five times before he reached the fence ahead of us. I should have hit him with the first shot, or at least with the second. With the third, he was getting out of range, and I fired the fourth and fifth shots mainly because I had two shells left in my shotgun. I learned two lessons from that experience. One, don't assume he's a dead rabbit just because he's in the open and you're holding a five-shot, pump-action, twelve-gauge shotgun. Two, if you're the rabbit, keep on running.

I kept on running, thinking after every missed shot that the next one would surely find its mark. But it never did. When I reached the woodlot on the other side of the field, I felt I was almost home free. Whoever was shooting at me, and I guessed that it was Whitey Huffer, he wouldn't want to cross an open field and give himself away. He'd have to find a way around it, which would give me time to get back to Pilkin's Knob where Jessie was parked.

Fortunately, I had parked Jessie pointing downhill because I was in no mood to play the "starting game" with her. When she sputtered and didn't start, I pushed in the clutch to start her rolling and then popped it when she'd built up some speed. She started then but not eagerly.

I drove without lights. If Whitey Huffer was still looking for me, I'd be a lot easier to spot with my lights on. The problem with driving without lights was that I had night blindness. Outside in the open I could see fairly well, but once inside a vehicle, I lost nearly all of my depth perception. I couldn't tell if the bright lights coming toward me were those of a UFO or a self-propelled combine; or if they were a quarter mile away or fifty yards away. The lights turned out to be those of Whitey Huffer's patrol car. He nearly hit me head on before I veered to one side.

I turned on Jessie's lights and tried to outrun him but gave that up when I slid on loose gravel and almost rolled Jessie over before I righted her again. By then Whitey Huffer had turned around and turned on his red light. If I continued on, I'd be resisting arrest, and he'd be well within his rights as sheriff to stop me anyway he could. The fear of being shot was enough to make me pull over to the side of Bear Hollow Road and stop.

Whitey slid to a stop behind me. He jumped out of his patrol car and ran up to Jessie with his gun in hand. "Get out," he yelled at me. "God damn you. Get out of the car."

As I opened the door to get out, he grabbed me by the

collar, spun me around, and slammed me up against Jessie. "Spread them," he yelled, then kicked me in the ankle right where I'd been hit. I felt a white hot flame shoot up my leg. My knees buckled, but I didn't go down.

He kept the barrel of his .44 Magnum jammed into my spine the whole time he searched me. Days later I could still feel it there, and the rage, fear, and total helplessness that had accompanied it. Anything could have set it off and I either would have been dead or paralyzed for life. For me, a man who loved both his life and his legs, it would have been a tough call which I would have preferred.

"What's this?" he said on finding the flashlight in the inside pocket of the sport coat.

"It's a flashlight."

"I'll bet." He took the flashlight from my pocket, saw what it was, and threw it into the bushes alongside the road.

"Sorry it wasn't a gun," I said.

"Shut up."

He jammed the barrel of the Magnum ever harder into my spine. Perhaps he hoped that it would accidentally fire. Or that I would flinch and make it fire.

"Give me your keys," he said.

"They're still in the ignition."

"Then get them for me."

He shoved me back into Jessie where I hit my nose on the steering wheel. Instantly tears of rage welled up in my eyes. I hated to hit my nose on anything. My nose hated to be hit on anything.

Once I had the keys in hand, he dragged me out of Jessie and shoved me toward her trunk. "Open it," he said.

I opened it then stood to one side while he went through it. Whitey Huffer had been drinking. I could smell the liquor on his breath.

He slammed the trunk lid down and made me stand with my hands on Jessie's roof while he searched inside. "What are you looking for?" I asked.

He didn't answer. But I guessed it was whatever he thought I had taken from the dump behind his house.

"It's not in there," I said.

He stopped searching long enough to point his gun at me. "What's not in there?"

"Whatever you're looking for."

"Don't play games with me, Ryland. I'm not in the mood."

"I'm not in the mood for this, either," I said.

"But you're not the one holding the gun."

"So I've noticed."

He turned away to continue his search.

"I think you need to sight your scope in," I said.

While at the dump, he hadn't shot at me with his .44 Magnum. The gun he'd used had sounded more like a .22 rifle, like the one that hung over his back door at home.

He stared blankly at me a moment as if he didn't know what I was talking about. I didn't think he was going to answer until he said, "You're lucky. That's all."

As I stood there with my hands on Jessie's roof with frozen fingers and a throbbing right ankle, I couldn't have agreed more.

Front seat, back seat, glove box, dashboard—he methodically took Jessie apart on the inside. I was impressed with his thoroughness and his control. It was a side of Whitey Huffer I had never seen before.

Then he reopened the trunk, took out the tire iron, and popped off all of Jessie's hubcaps. I didn't know what he hoped to find, but one thing was certain. If he had found the toaster oven with the vial of white power inside, he probably wouldn't have had to look any further. Even if he decided not to press charges, I and the *Oakalla Reporter* would have then belonged to him. The thought was enough to sicken me.

"Okay, where is it?" Whitey said. Once more he pointed his .44 Magnum at me.

"Where is what?" I lowered my arms and began to flex my fingers to get the feeling back in them.

"Don't give me any more of your crap, Ryland. You have something of mine and I want it."

He wasn't going to take no for an answer. If I didn't tell him what he wanted to know, I couldn't predict what he might do. All I had was Amel Pilkin to go by.

"If you're talking about your toaster oven," I said, "I left it back in the woods."

He didn't react the way I thought he would. Except for a look of puzzlement, he didn't react at all. "What in the hell are talking about?" he said.

"Your toaster oven," I repeated. "You shot a hole in it back in the woods."

"What in the hell would I want with a toaster oven?"

The fire and the booze had started to wear off. Instead of a raging demon or even a methodical lawman, Whitey Huffer was starting to look like a tired old drunk.

I did some quick calculations and decided that the less I said about the toaster oven the better. It obviously didn't belong to Whitey Huffer. Whoever it did belong to was probably better served with silence.

"My mistake," I said.

But Whitey Huffer didn't buy it. Even a tired old drunk could still be cunning. And mean. "Explain yourself, Ryland."

"I saw the toaster oven there in your dump, it looked like new, so I decided I might give it to Ruth for Christmas, since we don't have one at home. But then you shot a hole in it, so it's not good for anything."

He didn't believe me. "One last chance before I blow you away." He cocked the hammer of the .44 Magnum.

"Then you'll never know what I know," I said. "Or who else knows what I know."

I studied him as he studied me and saw why Whitey Huffer was losing so much money at poker. He was easy to bluff and easy to read. He wasn't going to shoot me, no matter what. That much I knew.

He lowered the hammer and put the Magnum back in its holster. I started to breathe a sigh of relief—until he traded his gun for his nightstick.

"Now what?" I said.

He smiled. Suddenly he didn't look like a tired old drunk anymore. He looked like the Whitey Huffer that I had come to know and hate.

"I'll teach you a lesson," he said. "It's Saturday night, remember?"

19

HOW COULD I have forgotten that it was Saturday
night, the very night that I had promised to fight Whitey
Huffer? Or rather, he had promised to fight me. But I had
forgotten all about it. Leave it to Whitey to jog my memory.

"What do I get to use?" I asked, moving away as he
moved toward me.

"Whatever you want to use," he said. "Out here, it's no
holds barred."

"What about your gun?" I said.

"Except that."

"Then empty it. So neither one of us will be tempted to
use it."

He stopped, took his Magnum out of its holster, and
emptied it. "Satisfied?" he said, putting it back in its holster.

"Now put your nightstick away."

He shook his head. "Sorry, Ryland. No can do."

"So what do I tell Claire afterward, that you weren't man
enough to fight me one on one? That you had to have help?"

I got a reaction but not the one I wanted. Instead of
throwing down the nightstick and charging me, he just
charged me with the nightstick in hand.

I tried to duck out of the way and to grab a handful of
gravel at the same time. He missed my head but caught me
squarely on the left shoulder. Immediately my left arm went
numb.

I threw the gravel at him and hit him flush in the face at

125

point-blank range. When his hands instinctively went to his eyes, I hit him in the stomach as hard as I could, doubling him over. Then I tried to kick him in the face, succeeded, but fell.

He scrambled on top of me and, using both his hands, pressed the nightstick against my throat. I still couldn't feel my left arm, only the weight of Whitey Huffer crushing my windpipe. I reached out with my right hand, found a small rock, and slammed it into his temple. He grunted and slumped forward just enough for me to roll out from under him.

We were both on our feet now, he stalking me with the nightstick in hand, I backpedalling while trying to get out of the sport coat. Some feeling began to return to my left arm, but still not enough for me to trust it. I needed to buy time while it recovered. Whitey Huffer, however, had other ideas.

"Why don't you stop and fight," he said, "instead of running away?" He kept stalking me. I kept backpedalling.

"When you drop your nightstick."

"Fair's fair," he said.

At last I managed to shed the sport coat. Wadding it up, I stopped and waited for him to take a step closer before I launched a chest pass at his head. He didn't have time to duck before it hit him. I saw my chance and went right for him with a hand shiver to his chest that knocked him off balance and made him drop his nightstick.

Before he could retrieve it, I hit him with a left hook to the chin that I intended to follow with a right cross. But the left hook dropped him. He didn't move once he hit the ground.

I picked up his nightstick, then stood at a safe distance away from him until I determined that he really was out cold and not playing possum. In boxing terms, Whitey Huffer had a glass jaw, which helped to explain why he didn't want to fight me with just his bare hands.

Whitey Huffer still lay on the ground after I had gathered up everything of mine that I could find. I had Jessie's hubcaps in her trunk, Amel's sport coat on the front seat beside me, and the front seat back in place, but that was it. The flashlight had never worked that well anyway, and I could put everything else back in place when I had time.

After checking Whitey's pulse to make sure he had one, I covered him with the army blanket from my trunk and took off. The first thing I did when I got home was to call Clarkie and tell him what had happened. The second thing I did was to call Claire Huffer.

"Your husband's lying unconscious along Bear Hollow Road about a mile southeast of your farm," I said through a folded handkerchief. "If I were you, I'd get your brother and go after him."

"Who is this?" she asked sharply.

"It doesn't matter who it is. Just do as I say, or he might freeze to death."

"I should be so lucky," she muttered.

Then Ruth returned from bowling before I had a chance to even hang up the phone. "What does Whitey Huffer look like?" was the first thing she said.

"Probably not as bad as I do."

She shook her head in disgust but said nothing more.

I went upstairs to clean up while Ruth took off her coat and put on a pot of coffee. Though I felt sore all over, including my back, chest, arms, legs, and neck, my right ankle, which still had something from the dump imbedded in it, hurt the worst. But it didn't hurt as badly as it would have had I lost the fight to Whitey Huffer.

When I went back downstairs again, Ruth poured my coffee and then set the sugar bowl and creamer in front of me. That was about all of the sympathy I could expect from her. She didn't give comfort unless comfort was absolutely needed.

"So what did you learn tonight?" she said.

"Whitey Huffer has a glass jaw."

"Besides that."

I told her.

The news disturbed her. "So somebody did unload Amel's pickup between the time he died and the time Orville Goodnight found him. And took Amel's coat in the bargain."

"That's the way it looks to me. I don't know how else Amel's coat could have gotten there."

"That still doesn't mean somebody killed Amel."

"No," I agreed. "It doesn't." Whitey Huffer had at least two golden opportunities to kill me and he hadn't, so that counted for something.

"Do you have any idea what it does mean?" she asked.

I had thought a lot about what had happened that night, and so far none of it made much sense to me. "No, Ruth, I don't know what it means. Maybe in time I will."

"Maybe in time you won't either."

I shrugged. The way I felt, it didn't much matter to me one way or another. A long time ago Doc Airhart had told me to let sleeping dogs lie. This time I should have listened to him.

Ruth and I had sat through two cups of coffee each when someone knocked on the front door. I looked at Ruth. She looked at me. We neither one were expecting company.

I opened the front door to see Clarkie there in full uniform. He appeared to be upset. In fact, I had never seen him so distraught.

"What's wrong, Clarkie?"

He stepped inside. He was so shaken he could hardly walk. "You know, Garth, how you wish for something and wish for something, all the time knowing that it will never come true. Well, it just came true. I'm now officially sheriff of Adams County."

"Whitey Huffer resigned?" I couldn't believe that.

"No, Garth. Whitey Huffer is dead. His wife called me just a few minutes ago to say that he shot himself."

I stared at him in disbelief, not knowing what to say.

"What's going on in there?" Ruth asked from the kitchen.

"Whitey Huffer just shot himself to death," I said when I could trust myself to speak.

"What next?" she said.

What indeed.

I dressed and then rode with Clarkie out to Claire Huffer's farm. "Garth, I'm going to need some help. I want to deputize you," he said as we pulled into the lane.

"You're too late, Clarkie," I said. "Rupert made me a special deputy years ago. I've got my badge somewhere at home. In the top drawer of my dresser, I think."

As I thought back on that event, which had occurred the night that I had given Rupert his first bottle of Crown Royal for Christmas, it seemed so free and innocent, so much a part of the past, as to have happened in my childhood.

"But you will act as my deputy?" Clarkie said.

"Until you can find somebody else."

Larry Stout's pickup was parked in the yard beside Whitey Huffer's patrol car. Buster Brown was inside the pickup. He barked at us as we walked by.

"You first," I said to Clarkie when we reached the back door. "I'm not sure how welcome I'll be anyway."

"That makes two of us."

We went in through the back door and then on into the kitchen where Whitey Huffer sat slumped in a chair facing the fireplace. Though coals and ashes by now, a fire still burned on the hearth. A bottle of Jack Daniel's and an empty water glass sat on the floor beside Whitey's chair. He wore his calfskin gloves, cowboy boots, and uniform, and clutched his .44 Magnum in his right hand. His brains and bits of his skull were sprayed on the sink and the window above it. He smelled as if he'd shit his pants.

Clarkie lasted just long enough to survey the scene before he excused himself and ran outside to vomit. I found a phone on the wall beside the kitchen door and called Ben Bryan. He said he was on his way.

I went into the living room where Claire Huffer and Larry Stout sat at opposite ends of the couch. A pink Gone-With-the-Wind lamp stood on the end table beside Claire with its lower light burning. Except for the one in the kitchen, it appeared to be the only light on in the house.

Claire wore a thin cotton nightshirt, what looked like Whitey's blood on the front of it, and a look of pure malice in her eyes. "What are you staring at?" she said. "Did you think I slept in my coveralls and gum boots?"

Larry Stout glanced from me to her and then back to me again. His look said that he, as well as his sister, blamed me for what had happened.

"Do you feel up to telling me about it?" I said to Claire.

"Why?" she said with tears in her eyes. "So you can gloat?"

"So Clarkie and I can fill out our report and then leave you in peace."

"If you wanted to leave me in peace, you would have started eight days ago," she said. "It's too late now."

I turned from her to her brother. "How about it, Larry?" I said. "Is that the way you feel, too?"

He shrugged. He really didn't have an opinion or care to share it if he did.

"The coroner will be here soon," I said to Claire. "You can tell him what you won't tell me."

"Why, Garth?" she said. "Why did you have to humiliate him so? Couldn't you have left him with his dignity at least?"

"How?" I said in anger, not really understanding the question. "By letting him beat the crap out of me tonight? I'm sorry, but that's not part of my job description."

"What exactly is your job, Garth?" Larry Stout said in that low, level, taciturn voice of his. "It's running that newspaper, isn't it?"

I expected him to continue. I should have known better. "I'll be outside," I said. "In case you need me."

"Why would I need you?" Claire answered bitterly. Then she added just for my benefit, "*Now.*"

I went outside to where Clarkie stood, staring at the stars.

He looked profoundly lonely standing there, like a man without a country. I walked over to him. He continued to stare at the stars.

"Are you okay, Clarkie?" I asked.

"I'm not cut out for this job, Garth," he said. "If I didn't know it before, I know it now."

"It's not always like this," I said. "In fact, most of the time it isn't."

He turned to look at me. There were tears of frustration in his eyes. "No," he said. "Most of the time it's husbands beating up on their wives or wives beating up on their husbands or husbands and wives beating up on their kids. Or drunks that want to pick a fight with somebody—anybody, it doesn't matter who. Or drunks that drive and end up killing somebody. Or perverts that just can't keep from calling somebody up on the phone. Or some lonely scared old woman who thinks somebody is crawling in her window. Or somebody's dog is missing or somebody's cat is dead. And I can't deal with those things, Garth."

He put his hands in his pockets and walked a few feet away where he stood with his back to me. I walked over to him and put my hand on his shoulder. He was close to breaking down, so I didn't say anything.

"As much as I hate to admit it," he said, "the people were right in electing Whitey Huffer sheriff. He could do all of the things I can't. Maybe not as well as Sheriff Roberts could but better than I ever will. So I'm going to turn in my resignation at the end of the month."

"At least wait until all of this is over," I said.

He turned to face me. "Until all of what is over?" he said, as his voice rang in anger. "It's over, Garth. Whitey Huffer is dead. You saw him. He blew his brains out all over his kitchen. So whatever he did or didn't do dies with him. As far as I'm concerned, this case is closed."

"It's not that easy, Clarkie. You're still sheriff, remember. You have an obligation to the people of Adams County to find out the truth and act on it."

"Truth?" he shouted. "Truth?" He pointed toward the house. "There's your God damned truth, Garth, Whitey Huffer with his brains blown out. I don't see how it can be much plainer than that."

I brushed past him and started walking. Within an hour, I was home.

20

SOMEONE ONCE SANG, "I didn't sleep at all last night." Neither did I that Saturday night. If my own bad thoughts hadn't kept me awake, the pain in my ankle would have.

Long before dawn, I got in Jessie and drove out to Pilkin's Knob where I parked facing downhill in exactly the same place that I had the night before. Then I sat there in the dark and the cold, waiting for the first light. When it came, I got out of Jessie and set out across country toward the ravine behind Claire Huffer's house.

As I approached it, I could hear the Holsteins bawling and the pigs squealing, as a flock of pigeons swept into the barn lot. I was reassured by the sound of bawling cows and squealing hogs. It meant that life on the farm went on. As long as life on the farm went on, so would the rest of us.

Things that look so large and foreboding at night often shrink in daylight. The ravine that I thought was at least ten miles long was no more than three hundred yards long, and neither as wide nor deep as the Grand Canyon. I found the toaster oven with the bullet hole in it at the north end of the ravine under a hackberry tree. The vial of white powder was still inside it.

I drove back to Oakalla and left the toaster oven at Clarkie's house while I went to see Doc Airhart. He didn't seem at all surprised to see me so early on a Sunday morning.

133

"Come in, Garth," he said. "You had breakfast yet?" Doc wore a maroon silk robe over his flannel pajamas and hard leather slippers that clacked as he walked.

"No," I said. "I haven't even had coffee."

"How do bacon and eggs sound?"

"Wonderful," I answered.

He bustled about the kitchen while I got a cup and poured my own coffee. Before I could even ask for it, he handed me a quart of milk from the refrigerator. "The sugar's already on the table," he said.

"How did you know I was coming?" I asked.

"Ruth called me a few minutes ago and said to expect you."

"How did Ruth know I was coming?" When I'd left home earlier that morning, she was sawing a redwood log.

"You'll have to ask her."

Doc fried a pound of bacon for the two of us, two eggs apiece, and fixed us each two slices of buttered whole wheat toast. We ate it all. There weren't even enough crumbs left to throw out to the birds.

"Do you eat like this every morning?" I asked.

"About," he said, mopping up the last bit of egg yolk with his last bite of toast. "How about you?"

"Only when Ruth cooks."

"Which is about how often?"

"About every other day."

"You should watch your cholesterol closer," he said with his mouth full of buttered toast and egg.

I rose to pour us another cup of coffee.

"So what's on your mind?" he asked, as I sat back down. "If you're wondering what Ben Bryan found out about Whitey Huffer, you'll have to ask him."

"That's not what I came for," I said. I set the vial of white powder on the table in front of him. "I'd like to know what this is, if you can tell me. I think it might be cocaine."

He picked up the vial to examine it. "Anything else?"

I pulled up my pants leg and pulled down my sock to

show him my ankle. "I've got something in there that I'd like for you to take out for me."

He bent down to examine my ankle, which, judging by the expression on his face, didn't look good to him. "Don't you have a regular doctor, Garth?"

"No. Not to speak of."

He felt my ankle until he located whatever was inside it. A sliver of glass, it felt like to me.

"That explains it then," he said. "I got a call from Byron Winters in Madison yesterday. He said you're going to be having surgery in a couple weeks. He seems to think I'm the one who referred you to him."

"Imagine that," I said.

He let go of my ankle. I put my foot down. "Yes," he said. "Imagine that."

We went into what used to be Doc's office where he found what he would need to work on my ankle. The office was about ten degrees colder than the kitchen and smelled like camphor. I lay on the examining table with my eyes closed and my pants leg pulled up to my knee. I could take about whatever pain Doc might dish out. I just couldn't watch while he did it.

"This might sting a little," he said as he numbed my ankle.

"Better than the alternative."

When he finished working on me, he said, "If I were you, I'd be lying down when the anesthetic wears off. I had to dig a little to get out some of the glass."

"I never felt a thing."

"You will," he promised.

I put my sock and shoe back on and hobbled out to the kitchen where I sat down again. Since I couldn't yet feel my right foot, I was having a hard time walking.

Doc took the lid off the vial of white powder, smelled inside it, then tasted the powder itself. "Well?" I said.

"I can't tell. I'll have to check it in my lab to know for sure."

"How long will that take?"

"Not long."

Doc went down to the basement where his lab was. I sat at the kitchen table, wriggling my toes, trying to feel my right foot. I wished Belle was still there to keep me company. I could imagine how lonely it was for Doc without her.

"Cocaine," Doc said on his return. I'd never seen him look so grim. "Where did you get it?"

"I found it in a toaster oven in a dump behind Whitey Huffer's house. I think it and the toaster oven were on Amel Pilkin's truck when he died."

"You have any idea who it belongs to?" he asked.

"Some," I said. "But I'm not yet ready to name names."

He capped the vial and set it back on the table. "You know what this does to your theory about Amel Pilkin, Garth? It shoots it all to hell. What I mean is, if Amel took a snort of that stuff before he went into the Corner Bar and Grill that Friday night, there's no telling how he might have acted."

I'd already thought of that possibility. High on cocaine, he could have acted exactly as he had, and I wouldn't have known the difference. "Then that envelope, or whatever it was that he showed me, could have had absolutely no meaning whatsoever."

"It and everything else, Garth," Doc said. "From his leaving the Corner Bar and Grill by way of the basement to his being found dead along the road."

"But wouldn't the cocaine have showed up in the autopsy?"

"Not necessarily. Not if you weren't looking for it, which Ben wasn't."

"It would also explain why Amel took off when he saw Whitey Huffer coming," I said. "As much as I don't like that explanation."

"What it doesn't explain," Doc said, "is why someone

would ever give it to Amel Pilkin in the first place. That borders on murder in my book."

"It had to be an accident," I said. "I can't think of anyone around here who would purposely do that to Amel."

Doc scowled. "It better have been an accident. That's all I can say."

21

BEN BRYAN MET me at his front door and let me inside. We went into his living room, a deep narrow room with high windows, high ceilings, white walls, and a hardwood floor, and sat down on the couch. We faced the fireplace. To its left was a staircase that led upstairs. Behind us were two large prints in gold frames. One I recognized as the "Blue Boy." The other was a group of fat angels in various stages of undress.

"Nice room," I said.

"I don't like it," Ben Bryan answered. "But my wife does."

Ben was dressed in a brown suit, brown wingtip shoes, and a brown-and-white striped tie. Apparently he and his wife, Faye, were about to leave for church.

"I won't keep you," I said.

"Keep me as long as you like." He winked at me. "You've heard one sermon, you've heard them all."

"That's not true, Ben Bryan," Faye Bryan said from upstairs. "You said yourself that you like Reverend Luke."

"Ears like a hawk," he whispered.

"I heard that, too," she said. "And it's eyes like a hawk."

"Not in your case."

A door slammed upstairs. We then had the living room to ourselves.

"It's like this, Garth," Ben said. "Whitey Huffer shot himself, plain and simple. The powder burns on his face and glove show it. The angle of entry shows it. The autopsy confirms it. What it doesn't tell, and maybe you can help me on this, is who beat him up before he shot himself."

"I did."

He nodded as if confirming something to himself. "That goes along with the rest of Claire Huffer's story then."

"What is the rest of her story?"

"I'm not sure I can tell you that, Garth."

"It's on line," I said. "Clarkie deputized me last night." I took out my wallet and showed him the badge that I had found in my dresser drawer. Though tarnished, it still looked official.

"So it is on line," he agreed after examining the badge.

I put the billfold back in my pocket and waited for him to continue.

"Claire Huffer's story is that she got an anonymous phone call, telling her that her husband was lying unconscious along Bear Hollow Road. She went there to find him sitting dazed in his patrol car. Apparently he'd been there for some time with the motor running because it was warm inside the car. But when she spoke to him, he didn't answer her. He just sat there staring out into space. Not wanting to leave him there like that, she drove him home in the patrol car, somehow got him inside the house, then called her brother, who drove her back to where she'd found Whitey to pick up her truck. Her brother then went on home, and she went on into the house where Whitey sat at the kitchen table, which is where she'd left him. But she said he had managed to take a bottle of Jack Daniel's out of the cabinet, even though he hadn't drunk any of it yet." He cocked his head as if listening for his wife to say something from upstairs. "Are you with me so far?"

"So far."

"The next thing Claire Huffer did was to build a fire in the fireplace, because, she said, Whitey liked to sit there in front of one whenever he had some thinking to do. It seemed to

relax him, she said, and Whitey usually didn't drink as much
with a fire going as he normally did. Then Whitey asked her
to get him a glass, which she did, and told her that she might
as well go on to bed because he was going to be there for a
while. She didn't argue because she'd been in the farrowing
house all evening with some sows that were having pigs,
and she was just about worn out. But she did stop to give
him a hug on her way to bed. He told her to sleep tight, or
something to that effect. Which she did until she heard the
gun go off and went into the kitchen to find him."

"Did he leave a note?" I asked

He reached inside his suit for the note and handed it to
me. "It's right here."

Well, Claire, I have made a mess of things, haven't I?
And you thought you were really getting something when
you married me. What a joke that turned out to be.

I've thought of all the ways I can undo this, all the
ways I can try to make things right, but nothing is going
to work. Your friend Garth Ryland has seen to that.

I had the chance to kill him tonight. I had my gun out
and the hammer cocked, but I couldn't pull the trigger.
Not even for you, Claire. So I'll leave him in your hands
to do what you will with him. Just don't screw him,
please, until at least after I'm buried.

My luck has run out, Claire. Or like the Big Man said
to me, I've crapped out for the last time. You'll have to
deal with him now and I don't envy you for that.

I love you, Claire. I know I haven't much acted like it,
and I'm sorry for that, but nobody's perfect, right? And
I'll miss you wherever I'm going.

But I won't miss my life, or the mess I've made of it.
I just wish things would've worked out different. But
then, doesn't everybody?

Your husband,
Whitey

The note had blood spots on it and what looked like a speck of flesh. I folded it and started to hand it back to Ben Bryan.

"You might as well keep it," Ben said. "I've got no further use for it."

I put the note in my shirt pocket. Ben Bryan looked at his watch.

"Was there anything else, Garth? We've got to leave here within the next ten minutes if we're going to make church on time."

"Five minutes," came the word from on high.

"Ten minutes is a God's plenty time to get to the Methodist Church," he said.

"Not the way you drive."

He stood and took his topcoat from the couch. "Come on, Garth," he said. "You can help me warm up the car."

We went out back to his garage, which housed all of Ben's garden tools and his tan Oldsmobile Eighty-eight. "What's wrong with the way I drive?" he muttered as he started the Oldsmobile. "It's better than the way she drives, which is not at all. If it weren't for me, she wouldn't even be going to church this morning. Or any morning, for that matter."

I sat with my head back on the plush seat, listening to the Oldsmobile purr. I had been driving Jessie for so long I had forgotten what a car was supposed to sound like. "Ben, do you remember what Amel Pilkin was wearing when you found him?" I asked.

He thought it over, then said, "Without going down into my basement to find out, I'd say blue jeans, long johns on under those, quilted shirt, quilted undershirt, and an insulated vest."

"But no plaid sport coat?" I thought that afterwards Whitey might have somehow coaxed it away from him.

"No plaid sport coat," he said with certainty. "I'd remember something like that."

"Is there any chance that Whitey Huffer could have taken the sport coat off of Amel before you got there?"

He turned on the defroster and put the fan on high. "Anything's possible," he said. "But I don't see how he would have had time since his dust hadn't settled by the time I got there. Why is the sport coat so important to you?"

"Amel was wearing it there in the Corner Bar and Grill the night he died. Then I found it rolled up and stuck in an old planter in the dump behind Whitey's house. Carolyn Fleischower said it used to belong to her father but that he gave up wearing it several years ago after her mother died."

"I think I remember that sport coat," Ben said with a smile. "Norman Fleischower used to wear it at all the political rallies just to draw attention to himself. Being a member of the opposition party, I always thought he looked like a jackass in it."

"Were he and Orville Goodnight friends?"

"Cronies would be a better word. Until Rupert Roberts came along, the two of them pretty much ran Adams County."

"Do a lot of people now in politics still owe Orville favors?"

He smiled at my ignorance. "It's hard to think of any who don't. The same held true for Norman Fleischower when he was alive."

"What about Warren Stout? Did he have any political clout?"

Ben turned the fan down a couple notches then said, "Not so you'd notice. He had money and money talks, but he didn't throw his weight around like the other two did, if that's what you mean."

"That's what I mean."

Faye Bryan rushed into the garage. She seemed to be running late, so I got out of the Oldsmobile so that she could get in.

"Before you go, Garth, I have a question for you," said

Ben. "Have you ever found Amel Pilkin and the stolen van he was riding in?"

"Didn't Clarkie tell you?"

"Tell me what?"

I watched as Faye Bryan hurriedly tried to buckle her seat belt. First she got it tangled in her coat, then in her purse. Finally Ben reached across her and buckled it for her.

"I could have gotten it myself," she said.

"I know that, dear."

"The stolen van is at the bottom of Hidden Quarry," I said. "Amel Pilkin's body is in it."

"We ought to just leave it there," he said.

"Except I need to have Amel's body tested for cocaine."

"Cocaine!" he exclaimed loudly enough for the whole east end of Oakalla to hear. "You can't be serious."

"I was never more serious." I closed the car door and watched them drive away.

Clarkie wasn't wearing his uniform. Instead he wore black loafers, white socks, jeans, and a black-and-white plaid button-down shirt that made him look like Howdy Doody.

As soon as he let me in, I went straight for Clarkie's couch. Doc Airhart was right when he said that I'd feel it when the anesthetic started to wear off. I felt it all the way from my knee to the sole of my foot. It felt like someone had taken a jackhammer to my leg.

"Something wrong with your leg, Garth?" Clarkie said as I gingerly lowered myself to the couch.

"Nothing that amputation wouldn't cure. What did you find out about the toaster oven?"

Clarkie sat down in the green overstuffed chair that matched his couch. He looked stiff and uncomfortable sitting there, as if this were a part of the house he rarely used.

"The toaster oven's not been reported stolen anywhere," he said. "At least it's not listed anywhere in the network."

"I guessed that much," I said, trying not to show my impatience with him. "What else did you find out about it?"

"What makes you think I found out anything else about it?" Already he was on the defensive.

"Because you're the sheriff now, damn it, whether you like it or not. And because I know you well enough to know that you wouldn't let it end there, no matter how sorry you felt for yourself."

"I don't feel sorry for myself," he insisted.

"Sure you do, Clarkie, just like I feel sorry for myself. My leg's killing me, Ruth's disgusted with me, and Claire Huffer hates me. I've already lost one good friend in Carolyn Fleischower and will probably lose some more before this is all over. Besides that, I feel guilty as hell for what happened to Whitey Huffer, and there's not Rupert Roberts around to bail me out of it, so I'm going to have to take my lumps and learn to live with it." I flipped Whitey Huffer's suicide note at him. "Here. Read this if you really want to feel sorry for yourself."

He left the suicide note lying on the floor in front of him. "What is it?" he said.

"Whitey Huffer's last words to his wife. If only the sonofabitch hadn't sat down in front of a fire and drunk a glass of Jack Daniel's before he wrote it, I might not feel so bad."

Clarkie picked up the note and read it before he threw it back at me. "Keep it," he said. "I don't want it."

"It's not mine to keep. It belongs to Claire Huffer." I put the note back in my pocket. Maybe someday I'd have the guts to return it to her. "Now, tell me what else you learned about the toaster oven," I said.

He sighed. What Clarkie could never do was lie, even when he wanted to. And he wanted to then, but his conscience wouldn't let him. "What I learned was that it was bought at the Five and Dime here in Oakalla at least five years ago."

"Had Harold seen it?" Harold Weaver was the owner of Oakalla's Five and Dime.

"He's seen it. He's checked the make, model, and serial number. It's one of his. But it has to be at least five years old because Harold said they discontinued that model five years ago because they were having so much trouble with it." Clarkie got up, went into his kitchen, and returned with the toaster oven. "Is there anything else you want to know?" he said.

"Does Harold have any idea who bought it?"

"No."

I tried to stand up, but because of the sudden pain in my foot, had to sit back down again. "Thanks, Clarkie, I'll be on my way in just a minute." I tried to stand up again and succeeded.

"Where are you going?" he asked.

"Orville Goodnight's. Do you want to ride along?"

He scowled at the mention of Orville Goodnight's name. "No. I don't want to ride along."

"If I were going anywhere but there?"

"No, Garth. I told you last night how I felt."

"You're still the sheriff. Don't forget that."

"How could I forget that?" he said bitterly. "It's what I always wanted to be."

22

THE DRIVE TO Orville Goodnight's farm seemed to take forever. By then my ankle hurt so badly that I couldn't think of anything else but it. I wished that after leaving Clarkie's house I'd gone home to bed. I wished I had never gotten out of bed in the first place.

Orville Goodnight sat on a bale of hay just inside his barn door. I sat down on the bale beside him. I could see his breath and mine stream out into the cold air. I could hear pigeons flutter and coo as they shuffled along the pulley track near the top of the barn. For the longest time that's all I heard.

"You know, Garth, what I miss most in this life?" Orville said. "It's my cows. I rue the day I ever sold them for slaughter. Life hasn't been nearly as much fun without them."

I thought back to what had happened to Norman Fleischower after his best friend and then his wife died. How most of the fun had then gone out of his life. And how sad Doc Airhart had looked the night that Belle died. And I wondered if that was the inevitable price of growing old. Someone had once said that we didn't stop playing because we grew old. We grew old because we stopped playing. Perhaps we stopped playing because, like Orville, Norman, and Doc, we ran out of playmates.

"You've got your nerve," Orville continued, "coming here today."

"I don't want to be here any more than you want me to be here."

"Then why are you here, Garth?"

I looked around the barn. It was a grey cold cloudy day outside, a dim cold musty day inside. "Because I want this to end with Whitey's death. I don't want anyone else to die."

"You should have thought of that before you stuck your big nose into things," he said.

Orville had his red leather cap pulled down low on his forehead, the collar up on his insulated coveralls, and his earflaps down over his ears and tied under his chin. About all I could see of him there in the dark barn were his nose and his eyes. His eyes glistened, like dim stars in a dusky sky.

"You should have thought of it before you decided to take the law into your own hands," I said. "Neither one of us is as innocent as we would like to be."

"I don't know what you're talking about," he said.

"I think you do, Orville. I think you called up the state fire marshal and claimed one of the favors he owed you. As a result, he put the lid on the investigation of the fire at Pilkin's Knob."

Orville stared straight at the barn's center support post on which the weight of the whole barn rested. "Why would I want to do a thing like that?" he said.

"Protecting someone."

"Like who?"

I took an educated guess. "Carolyn Fleischower."

When he didn't say anything, I knew I'd guessed right. "Why would I want to protect Carolyn?" he said after a minute.

"Because she's the one who set fire to Pilkin's Knob."

"You'll have a hard time proving that in a court of law," he said.

"Is that where you want to end up?"

"You know better."

"Then tell me what you know and maybe it won't have to."

He turned to look at me. I could see the doubt in his eyes. "If I tell you what I know, it can't do anything else but end up there."

"Not if it's off the record," I said, suddenly unsure of the ground on which I stood. As a newspaperman, I had every right to keep sensitive information confidential. As acting deputy sheriff, I might not only have no right to keep the information to myself, but I might be committing a felony by doing so. "On second thought," I continued, "don't tell me. Let me tell you."

"Fair enough," he said, looking relieved.

"My guess is that Carolyn Fleischower didn't set out to burn down Pilkin's Knob. The only reason she went there was to try to recover something that she thought she might have thrown away by mistake. Don't ask me what it was because I don't know. I don't even know if she did throw anything away by mistake. When she arrived to find me already there at Pilkin's Knob, she panicked. I might have, too, under the same circumstances. She got her car stuck and had to let me pull her out. But instead of then going home, she came here. Maybe she just wanted to sit for a few minutes to calm herself down before driving home. Then she saw your gas pump and thought she'd found a solution to her problem. Whatever was there on Pilkin's Knob, whether real or imagined, wouldn't be there any longer if the place burned down. So she found a gas can, filled it with gas, and drove back to Pilkin's Knob where she set fire to everything there. But you had seen her either coming or going from here and guessed the worst once the fire broke out."

We sat in silence for a while, listening to the pigeons flutter and coo. "How did you decide on Carolyn?" he asked. "Why not Raymond Fleischower or Larry Stout or Whitey Huffer for that matter? They all drove by here at one time or another that day. I haven't seen so much traffic along Bear Hollow Road since before the flood took the bridge out in 1957."

"When was Whitey Huffer by here?" I knew about the others but not about him.

"First thing last Sunday morning. I was out picking up my Sunday paper when he drove by."

"That was the only time you saw him that day?"

"Yes, except for later at the fire. But that doesn't mean he couldn't have sneaked by here and started the fire. Or Raymond Fleischower or Larry Stout, for that matter."

"But Raymond and Larry would both know that Amel kept kerosene around for his lamps," I said in their defense. "Why bring in gasoline when there was a drum of kerosene there and all the cans, bottles, and plastic jugs you would ever need to distribute it?"

"That still leaves Whitey Huffer," Orville said.

"But would Whitey be stupid enough to leave the gasoline can there after he torched the place?"

"It wouldn't make much sense at that," Orville agreed.

"Not unless your heart was leading your head, which would have been the case with Carolyn Fleischower."

We sat for a while longer. My ankle actually felt better there in the cold barn than it had in the warmth of Clarkie's house. That was because both of my feet were numb.

"I have another question, Orville," I said. "On the night that Amel died, do you remember seeing or hearing his truck drive by here on his way home?"

Orville smiled at me. "I've been wondering for over a week when someone would get around to asking that question. Yes. I did hear Amel's truck drive by here on its way home a week ago Friday night. That was why I was so surprised to see it parked along the road the next morning."

"You're sure it was Amel that went by here?"

"Garth," he said. "I've been watching him drive that thing back and forth from home for years. I know what it looks like, what it smells like, and what it sounds like, particularly when it's loaded, like it was that Friday night. I can hear it coming a mile away."

"But it wasn't loaded when you found it the next morning," I said. "Didn't that seem strange to you?"

"Not if Amel unloaded it once he got home and then took off again, which I assumed he did."

"But that was all you saw," I said, wanting to make sure. "Just Amel's pickup go by that one time."

"Yep. That's all I saw. I wouldn't have seen that if I hadn't been outside heeding the call of nature. Being a country boy, I never have got used to peeing indoors. Seems like a waste of good water to me."

"Thanks, Orville," I said. "You've been a big help."

"But too late, I'm afraid, to save Whitey Huffer," he said with regret. "Now I've got to put up with that beach ball Clarkie for the next four years. If I should live so long."

"Not so," I said. "Clarkie plans to resign at the end of the month."

"What for?" he said.

"He doesn't think he's up to the job."

"He isn't," Orville agreed.

23

CAROLYN FLEISCHOWER LET me in the back door, led me into the kitchen, then excused herself. I had hobbled from Orville Goodnight's barn to Jessie, driven to Carolyn's house, and then hobbled to her back door where I waited for her to answer my knock. She was a long time in coming. And when she saw who it was, she almost turned around and went the other way.

"What do you want, Garth?" she had asked through the door.

Her face was puffed, her eyes were red and swollen, and she carried a box of Kleenex in her hand. She looked as if she had been crying most of the morning.

"I need to talk to you," I said.

"What about? If it's about Whitey, you're wasting your time."

"It's not about Whitey. It's about you."

So there I sat in the kitchen, waiting for her.

The kitchen had changed from when I first knew it. Cabinets and a built-in stove had been added, along with new linoleum and new wallpaper. The door between the kitchen and the living room had been enlarged and a roughhewn beam inserted above the door. The refrigerator and the sink looked new, and the microwave oven definitely was new, since as long as he was alive, Norman Fleischower wouldn't allow one in the house. But even with all of the

151

changes, the house still felt the same to me—warm, drowsy, and secure.

Carolyn Fleischower returned wearing a thick orange terry robe over her housecoat. She had brushed her hair and put on some orange rouge and orange lipstick. She looked good in orange, one of the few people I knew who did.

"I see you're still here," she said.

"Still here."

She sat down heavily on the chair across from me, took out a cigarette from the pack on the table, and lighted it. I sat twiddling my thumbs while she sat smoking her cigarette. The air in there was thick with things unsaid.

"I am sorry about Whitey," I said to break the ice.

"Are you really?" she answered, not trying to hide her anger. "It's a bit late for that, isn't it?"

"Better late than never."

She mashed out her cigarette so hard that she scooted the ashtray halfway across the table. "Not in this case. So say what you came for, and don't pretend feelings that you don't have."

I said what I'd come for. When I finished, Carolyn Fleischower didn't look much different than when I started. If anything, her anger at me had hardened.

"You'll never prove it," she said.

"I don't want to prove it. I don't need to prove it. I know it. That's all that matters."

She lighted another cigarette, then scooted her chair back away from the table and crossed her legs. She was in control. She made it a point to let me know that.

"So what do you plan to do, blackmail me?" she said. "You won't get much. I can promise you that. Because there's not that much to get."

I pictured how she had looked naked. There was more to get than she knew.

"I want you to tell me what you thought you were destroying by burning Pilkin's Knob."

She blew a stream of smoke my way. "I don't know what

you're talking about, Garth. I've never been to Pilkin's Knob."

"You were there the day of the fire. Twice, if I recall."

"Besides then."

"And Amel wasn't wearing your father's sport coat the night he was killed?"

The question hit home, though she tried not to let it show. "The night he *died*, Garth. Nobody has said anything about Amel being killed."

"Okay," I said. "We'll have it your way. So Amel wasn't wearing your father's sport coat the night Amel died?"

"I don't know anything about any sport coat," she said smoothly between her drags on her cigarette, acting as if we had never spoken about it. "As far as I know, Dad's sport coat is still in his closet."

"It's out in Jessie," I said. "Would you like me to show it to you?"

"No," she said, losing some of her composure. "I wouldn't."

"Who are you protecting?" I asked. "It still can't be Whitey. He's dead."

At the word "dead," tears welled up in her eyes. She looked away, then took a long deep drag on her cigarette. "Why can't it be Whitey?" she said, regaining her composure. "Am I supposed to stop loving him just because he's dead."

"Open your eyes, will you," I said, suddenly angry at her. "Whitey and Claire were up to their ears in debt over Whitey's gambling. And Whitey has a little sweetie over at the bank in Madison who misses him just as much as you do. I didn't do the man any favors, but he didn't do himself many, either. He was walking a tightrope, Carolyn. It was only a matter of time before he fell off."

She turned to look at me. She hated even the sight of me. "But you're the one who pushed him over the edge," she said. "I can never forgive you for that."

"Then don't forgive me, if that's the way you want it. Just tell me what Amel had that Whitey was after."

"I don't know," she shouted. "I don't know. I don't know. I don't know." She rose and beat her fists on the table. "I don't know. Do you hear me? I don't know."

"Do you have a guess?"

She looked as if she wanted to spit in my face. "Jesus, Garth, you're really something, you know that. Where do you get your nerve? That's what I want to know. Where in the hell do you get your nerve?"

"Then order me out of your house," I said. "If I offend you so."

I had tried to bluff her. She called my bluff.

"There's the door," she said. "Use it."

I rose and slowly put some weight on my right foot, as a thousand needles jabbed me all at once. "If you change your mind about what you know, give me a call," I said.

"Okay, Garth," she said. "Just what *do* I know?"

"I won't know until you tell me."

"You see," she said triumphantly. "You're not as smart as you want me to think you are. You're just a bluff, Garth. One great big bad bluff."

"Remember what I said. Give me a call when you feel like talking."

"That'll be a cold day in hell."

"Whatever day is fine with me," I said on my way out.

Once I reached Jessie, I sat there for a while, waiting for the pain in my foot to subside. Two down and one to go.

24

FROM THE ROAD, I could see Raymond Fleischower skating on his pond. He made a lap around it, then turned around and skated backwards, never once breaking his rhythm or looking the least bit awkward. I admired his grace and ease. He seemed contented, a man at peace with himself.

By the time I had made the long walk back to the pond, I felt sick to my stomach. So I sat down on the frozen ground and bent over with my head between my legs until the sickness went away.

Raymond skated over to where I sat. "Is something wrong, Garth?"

"Morning sickness."

He smiled. "I should have known."

He skated away, took a couple laps around the pond, and returned to sit on the ground beside me. Large, dry, Wheaties-sized snowflakes fell a few at a time, dusting the pond and the ground around us. We had the pond to ourselves.

"I suppose you heard about Whitey Huffer," I said.

"Yeah. Sis called Carla the first thing this morning. She was taking it pretty hard."

"You knew about her and Whitey?"

He dug out a rock with his skate and threw it. "There weren't many people out this way who didn't know," he said. "I didn't like the idea, but there wasn't much I could do about it. Carolyn's an adult. She has to lead her own life."

"Your father never would have stood for it."

He dug out another rock and threw it. This one bonged the ice, then scooted on across the pond. "My father would never have stood for a lot of things that have been going on around here lately. If he were still alive, none of us would be in the mess we're in."

"I take it that includes you?"

"You can take it any way you like."

"Do you have any idea why I'm here today?" I said.

Raymond Fleischower was a class act. He showed me how much class he had when he said, "You've probably come to save my soul. And my marriage along with it."

"I didn't know your marriage was in trouble."

"Then you don't know as much as I think you do."

"I found the cocaine in your toaster oven, if that's what you mean," I said.

"How do you know it's my cocaine?" he said without a smile.

"It's your toaster oven. Since it's my guess that Carla was the one who threw it out, I assume that it was your cocaine inside it." Then I remembered that I wasn't just Raymond Fleischower's friend. I was acting deputy sheriff of Adams County, Wisconsin. "But don't answer that. Because I really don't want to know."

He turned my way. His eyes said he was in pain. "Somebody has to know, Garth. Somebody has to stop me, or it's going to go on and on. Because I can't stop myself. I've tried."

"Try again."

"Easy for you to say."

"Get help this time. Real help. Admit yourself someplace, and don't come out again until you're clean."

He shrugged, as if he really didn't believe that there was help out there for him. Sometimes the smarter we were, the dumber we were, because we smart ones believed we were unique in our pain. Raymond Fleischower was no exception.

"You know, it's funny, Garth," he said. "For nearly five years that toaster oven's sat broken in our garage, waiting to go to the dump. Why on that Friday, of all days, would Carla decide to give it to Amel?"

"Maybe to teach you a lesson."

"I thought of that. But she swears she didn't know what was in it."

"But you say your marriage is in trouble. How could she not know, Raymond?"

He then set me straight. "Oh, she knows I use the stuff. She just doesn't know where I keep it."

"Maybe she made it a point to find out."

He thought for several seconds before he said, "Why?"

"That's not so hard to figure out. She might just love you. She might even want to spend the rest of her life with you. But not with an addict."

"Is that what I am?" He didn't take me seriously.

"That's what you are, like it or not."

"I don't feel like an addict."

The large light flakes of snow continued to fall. But I could see the sun through the clouds.

"Answer me this question, Raymond. Did Whitey Huffer know that the cocaine was in the toaster oven?"

He laughed at the thought. "What do you think, Garth? Whitey and I were friends, but not that good friends."

"So whatever Whitey might have been after had nothing to do with you."

"Absolutely nothing to do with me," he said. "I can guarantee you that."

"Do you know what Whitey was after?" I asked.

"To be honest, Garth, I didn't even know Whitey was after anything. But you could ask sis. She might know."

"I did ask her. She knows, but she won't tell me."

"Then you might as well forget it," he said. "Once sis

makes up her mind about something, it usually stays made up."

We both rose at the same time, neither one of us gracefully. But then my right foot felt as if it had fallen off and Raymond was wearing ice skates.

"How many people know about Whitey's gambling debts?" I said to see what he'd say.

"Just the family."

"You're not family," I pointed out.

"The same as. Come to Whitey's funeral on Wednesday. You'll see. Sis and Claire will be crying in each other's arms, just like at Warren's funeral and then at Dad's. They won't let a little thing like adultery come between them."

"Share and share alike, huh?"

"Everything but the Stout farm. That belongs to Claire. Make no mistake about that."

"And Larry," I said. "Half of it belongs to him."

"In name only." He wobbled back onto the ice where he turned to face me. "That vial of cocaine you found," he said. "You didn't by any chance bring it with you?"

"It's in my pocket. Why?"

"It belongs to me."

"I didn't hear that, Raymond. You didn't say it."

"What I meant was, if it happened to fall out of your pocket, who would be the wiser?"

"I would."

"I could make it worth your while."

I'd found something that hurt more than my ankle. "You're not serious, are you?"

He smiled. But it lacked its usual warmth. "You be the judge." He turned and skated away.

I started the long walk back to Jessie. When I was about halfway there, Carla Fleischower came out of the house to help me the rest of the way. I was grateful for her help. I doubted that I could have made it without her.

"What did Raymond have to say?" she asked, as she got

in the passenger side door and sat down on Jessie's front seat.

She wore tennis shoes, jeans, and a thin leather jacket over whatever she had on underneath it. She didn't look dressed for the cold.

"What did Raymond have to say about what?" I said.

"Anything."

"He said of all days he couldn't understand why you picked a week ago Friday to throw out his stash of cocaine."

She bit her lip and didn't say anything.

"I said maybe it was to teach him a lesson. Was that the way it was?"

"Yes," she said. "I was desperate. I didn't know what else to do."

"Why didn't you just file for divorce?"

She stopped biting her lip. "I couldn't do that. What would Raymond ever do without me? More to the point, what would I ever do without Raymond? He's my life, Garth. I wouldn't even want to try to make it without him."

I started Jessie. Just because her heater hadn't worked the past eight weeks in a row didn't mean it wouldn't work now.

"I don't know, Carla, what you would ever do without him. But what are you going to do with him if he doesn't break his addiction?"

She shook her head. She didn't want to listen. "I don't think it's gone that far."

"I think it has." I took the vial of cocaine out of my pocket. "But if you think I'm wrong . . ." I opened her hand, put the vial inside it, and then closed her fingers over the vial. "Go offer this to Raymond and see what he does."

She stared at me as if I had horns growing out of my head.

"It's okay," I said. "It's his. It's already bought and paid for."

She drew back her arm and threw the vial at me. Then she got out of Jessie and ran for the house. I had to lean all the way across the seat to close the door.

25

WHITEY HUFFER'S FUNERAL was held on Wednesday at two p.m. in the Lutheran Church. I didn't go.

On Wednesday at three p.m. I got in Jessie and drove to Fair Haven Cemetery where I parked a prudent distance from the mourners. It was a cold, grey windy day, like the three days that had preceded it. I couldn't remember when I had last seen the sun.

Raymond Fleischower was right when he said that Claire Huffer and Carolyn Fleischower would cry in each other's arms. They stood arm in arm as Whitey Huffer's casket was lowered into the ground; then each knelt and placed a rose on top of it; then Raymond Fleischower approached his sister and led her away.

I walked down from the hill behind Claire Huffer to stand beside her. She, Larry Stout, the mortician, and I were the only ones left in Fair Haven Cemetery. Jessie, and the hearse, and Larry's green Ford pickup were the only vehicles in sight.

"We have to talk," I said.

"So talk," she said, without looking at me.

"Not here. And not now. But sometime soon."

She glanced at Larry Stout, who was leaning on the Stout family headstone, looking off into the distance. "Larry, do you mind driving home alone?" she said.

"No. I don't mind."

"Then I'll ride with Garth."

Larry and the mortician left. I went to Jessie to wait for Claire. When I saw her coming, I got out of Jessie and opened the door for her.

"Thank you," she said once we were inside.

"You're welcome."

She wore a long black coat over a long black dress, black heels, red lipstick, and gold earrings. She looked beautiful, more beautiful than I had ever imagined she could look.

"Is something wrong?" she said, as I sat staring at her.

"No. I've just never seen you dressed up before."

She leaned back on Jessie's seat and closed her eyes. "Then that makes us even. I've never buried a husband before."

I started Jessie. Then we rode in silence through Oakalla and on out to her farm. I was always amazed at the change that took place in Oakalla and the surrounding countryside between June and November. In June, Oakalla came into its fullness, and every bush, tree, flower, and fern was flush and fat. In November, when the last leaf fell, you saw what you hadn't seen since earliest spring, which were the bare bones of winter. It often made me wonder which was the real Oakalla, June or November?

As we drove up the long winding lane to Claire Huffer's house, I could feel her withdraw even further into herself. I thought about the first time I had driven up that same lane to interview her for my article in the *Oakalla Reporter*. It had been summer then, or late spring. A softer kinder time, as I remembered.

I parked Jessie near the back door. We got out and walked into the house where I stopped in the kitchen, and Claire kept on going on into the house. The kitchen felt cold to me. A fire would help to warm things up, so I made one.

Claire returned in the same black dress she had been wearing, but without her shoes, hose, and earrings. She had also taken the black ribbon from her hair. Her hair was really closer to orange in color than anything else, though no one would ever have called her a carrot top.

"The fire feels good," she said, pulling up a chair next to it. It was the same chair that Whitey Huffer had been sitting in when he shot himself.

I pulled up another chair and sat beside her. She was right. The fire felt good.

"I'm sorry," I said, wanting to get it off my chest.

"For what?" She extended her feet to warm her toes.

"For what happened to Whitey. I didn't know how close to the edge he was. Or I wouldn't have pushed him so hard."

"That goes for both of us," she said while staring into the fire. "So don't put all of the blame on yourself."

Then she rose from the chair, went to her kitchen cabinet, and returned, carrying a bottle of Jack Daniel's and two old-fashioned glasses. "Don't worry," she said, handing me a glass. "It's not the same bottle that Whitey used. Or the same glass. I threw them both out."

"But not the chair," I said.

"No. Not the chair."

I held out my glass, and she half-filled it with Jack Daniel's, then did the same with her glass. "A toast," she said, raising her glass.

"To what?"

"Beginnings and endings."

I touched my glass to hers. "I'll drink to that. God knows I've seen enough of them."

She sat warming her feet. I sat watching the fire. Never would I outgrow my fascination with fire, not if I lived to be a hundred.

"You said we needed to talk," she said.

"So I did," I said, hating to break the mood.

"What do we need to talk about?" She ran her bare foot over my sore ankle, but it didn't hurt much. "I thought it all had been said."

I set down my glass and turned my chair toward her. She put her feet in my lap, and I began to massage them.

"We need to talk about what drove Whitey to his death," I said. "Among other things."

Her face had begun to soften. Her eyes were nearly closed. I reached out and began to massage her calves.

"I thought we'd both taken equal blame for Whitey's death," she said. "Why hit ourselves over the head with it?"

Then I smelled her perfume and began to feel all of the things that I'd promised myself that I wouldn't feel that day. "Because I don't think we're entirely to blame," I said. "He mentioned the Big Man in his suicide note. Was the Big Man putting the squeeze on you? Is that why you have to sell the land to Bench-Mart, to pay him off?"

Her eyes opened momentarily, then closed again. "You don't miss a trick, do you? No wonder Whitey felt doomed the moment you got involved."

Her calves were soft and firm; the tension in them began to give way to the pressure of my hands. I could imagine what the rest of her would feel like.

"But am I right? Was the Big Man putting the squeeze on you over Whitey's gambling debts?" I slid my chair closer to hers.

"Yes," she said. "He was putting the squeeze on us over Whitey's gambling debts. And that's why I have to sell the land to Bench-Mart."

"How much do you owe him?"

"Over two hundred thousand dollars. More than I can afford to borrow at this time."

More than I could afford to borrow ever. "How did Whitey get in so deep?"

I felt her stiffen and pull away from me. She opened her eyes and sat up in her chair. "By not stopping when he should have," she said. "Something that we all can take a lesson from."

I started to massage her feet again. She fought it at first but then gradually began to relax.

"Would it help if I went to the Big Man and told him to forget the debt?" I said.

"Do you know who he is?"

"I think so."

"Then who is he?" She didn't believe I knew.

I told her.

She stared at me in amazement. Her eyes were bright and warm. "How do you find out these things?"

I tapped my temple with my forefinger. "Kidneys."

"I bet." She frowned at me. "But no, I don't want you going to him on my behalf. I don't want you going after him at all."

"Why? Has he threatened you?"

"Yes. He's threatened me."

"With what?"

"Nothing specific. Vague threats, like what might happen if all of our creditors suddenly called in their loans. Or what might happen if our farrowing house should burn down with all of our sows in it. Or what if our cattle developed some mysterious disease, and we had to destroy the herd." Her voice was hard and brittle. "There's no end to the things that you can threaten a farmer with."

"And you believe him?"

I was certain that the Big Man, as Whitey called him, had helped to steal the van and Amel Pilkin's body. But I wondered how much he would risk outside of Madison. Stealing a van and a body was one thing. Destroying someone's livelihood was another—particularly when there was nothing to gain by it. So the odds were that he was bluffing her.

"I can't afford not to believe," she said. "I have too much to lose."

"So when you sell the land to Bench-Mart and pay the Big Man off, then what?"

Her smile was bittersweet. "I'll cross that bridge if, and when, I get to it."

"Why wouldn't you get to it?" I said, feeling some alarm.

She shrugged. "There are no guarantees in life. Remember? You've said so yourself."

I looked away from her, back into the fire, which had

started to fall. "I was talking about somebody else. Not you and me."

"We're always talking about somebody else, Garth," she said gently, "when it comes to death."

I should have left. I had more than enough to do back at my office. But I knew I wouldn't leave until she told me to go.

"What?" she said. "I can almost hear your wheels turning."

"Nothing," I lied.

"Un-huh," she said, not believing me.

"It's about Whitey," I said. "And Amel Pilkin."

She looked disappointed. I wished then that I hadn't said anything. "What about Whitey and Amel?"

"Do you know if Whitey killed Amel or not, and if he did, why?"

She put her feet down and reached for her glass of Jack Daniel's. Already I missed the feel of her.

"Why would Whitey want to kill Amel?" she asked.

"That's what I'm asking you. You did know that the trash that Amel picked up on that last Friday ended up in the dump behind your house?"

"I knew," she said dully. "Whitey told me as much."

"But not why it was there?"

She shook her head no. "I don't even know that Whitey's the one who put it there."

"Who else could have put it there?"

"Larry could have. Or I could have."

"But you didn't."

Again she shook her head no.

"So that leaves Larry or Whitey. And I'm betting on Whitey."

She didn't say anything.

"Why won't you tell me what it was that he was after?" I said.

Her eyes opened wide in anger. "Because I don't know what it was that he was after," she said. "The first thing I knew about it, Whitey came home late that Friday afternoon and asked if Amel had been here to pick up the trash. I said he'd have to check the trash because I'd been in town all afternoon. When I asked him what was wrong, he said that nothing was wrong and left." She turned toward the fire. "That was the last I saw of Whitey until much later that night."

"How much later?"

"I don't know," she said. "I wasn't watching the clock."

The fire had burned down to coals. I went outside to the woodpile, brought in another armload, and added it to the fire. Soon the fire began to blaze again.

I turned my chair toward the fire to warm my hands. Ever since I had fallen through the ice at Willoby's Slough, my hands couldn't take the cold the way they used to. For that matter neither could the rest of me.

"You build a good fire," she said.

"Thank you. I think I'll have them put that on my tombstone. 'He built a good fire.' There are worse epitaphs."

She nodded, but didn't say anything.

"I've overstayed my welcome," I said. "I forgot you buried your husband today." I stood, preparing to leave.

"I don't want to be alone again, Garth," she said, her gaze on the fire. "I don't ever want to be alone again."

"Then don't be," I said.

She rose and came to me. I put my arms around her and gathered her in. She felt warm and soft and very good.

"We've done about enough talking for one day, don't you think?" she said.

When I didn't answer, she knew what I thought.

26

A WEEK PASSED. The weather went from cloudy and cold to fair and mild, as one quiet blue day followed another in what I hoped would be an endless procession into spring. But the weatherman said a change was coming Thanksgiving day when an arctic cold front would move across the state. High winds, snow squalls, steady to falling temperature—I'd heard it all before.

In that same week I'd been out to see Claire Huffer twice more. Each time, like the day of Whitey Huffer's funeral, I had intended to stay only a couple of hours and ended up spending the night. Each morning I awakened to find Claire Huffer entwined with me, and I would lie there holding her until she moved. Then I would move.

I wasn't used to that. I was used to getting up and going the minute I awakened. Or lying there in peace, planning my day. I wasn't used to waking up in someone else's bed and stumbling through someone else's house on my way to the bathroom. Or keeping someone else's schedule. Or being someone else's hero.

Claire had said to me that night on the kitchen floor after we made love for the first time, "Now your triumph over Whitey Huffer is complete."

Hail the victor! Just what I wanted to hear.

Only moments before I had lain there thinking, "God, this is too good to be true. Where are You hiding the rock that You are about to drop on my head?"

Then He dropped it, and things hadn't been quite the same since.

"So what are your plans today?" Ruth asked.

We sat at the kitchen table, drinking coffee. Breakfast was over and my workday about to begin.

"To get as much done as possible before tomorrow," I said.

Since tomorrow was Thanksgiving, I planned to have the *Oakalla Reporter* ready to print by that morning, so that Ruth and I could enjoy a leisurely Thanksgiving dinner together. Then I would return to my office that evening and make any last minute changes before I called in my printer, Cecil Edwards. That is if things worked out. Usually my last minute changes took hours.

"So that means you plan on eating here tonight."

Twice within the past week, Ruth had fixed suppers that I hadn't eaten. She wouldn't fix a third.

"Yes. I plan on eating here tonight," I said. "And for sure I'll be here for dinner tomorrow."

She took a drink of her coffee and set her cup down. "Why? Did you tell Claire Huffer that you had other plans?" She looked me right in the eye. "Or weren't you invited for Thanksgiving dinner?"

"I wasn't invited."

Though she didn't show it, I could tell that Ruth was smiling inside. "I'm sorry to hear that."

"I'll bet." I rose and went to the window, steamed and orange with the sun's first rays.

"Is something bothering you, Garth?"

"Yes. Something's bothering me." Though I had tried to put it out of my mind, it was the same something that had been bothering me since the night that Whitey Huffer shot himself. I told her what it was.

"I see," she said, mulling it over. "But it was dark that night. He might not have recognized the coat."

"Maybe not," I said. "Still I wonder."

A short time later I walked to work. The sun was up, the

morning cool and still. Almost a spring morning by the feel of it.

Clarkie was parked there at the *Oakalla Reporter*, waiting for me. He got out of his patrol car and followed me into my office where he sat in the same seat that Rupert always used to sit in when he came into the office. And like Rupert, he took off his sheriff's hat, adjusted the brim, and set it in his lap. If he had taken out his tobacco pouch and put a chew into his mouth, the picture would have been complete. And I wouldn't have felt so alone.

"I just wanted to thank you, Garth," he said, "for standing by me over the years. And thank you once again for putting in a good word for me in the *Reporter*. But my mind's made up. Three more days and that's the end of it."

"Has the County Council found anyone to take your place yet?" I said.

"Not yet. But they're looking."

"They've only got three days," I said. "They'd better find someone soon."

"That's what I keep telling them. But to a man they seem to think that I'm going to change my mind."

"And there's no chance of that?" I said hopefully.

"No chance," he said, though I thought he wavered a little.

Glancing at the mock-up of Friday's *Oakalla Reporter*, I saw that I had even more to do than I'd thought. "What are you going to do?" I asked. "Or do you know yet?"

"The state police have offered me a job manning one of their computers. I think I'm going to take them up on it."

"You'd be good at that."

"I know," he said without enthusiasm. He rose and put his sheriff's hat back on. "Well, that's about it. I just wanted to say thanks for all that you've done for me. And to say that I'm sorry I'll never get the chance to repay the favor."

I rose and offered my hand. He shook it warmly.

"Never say never, Clarkie. Life has its way of making liars out of us all."

He left and I went to work.

It was late afternoon. I was about to call Ruth to tell her that I wouldn't be home for supper after all when I saw Clyde Beaman, one of Oakalla's two rural mail carriers, drive by on Gas Line Road on his way back to the post office. After he'd passed, I stood at the window for the longest time, wondering how I could have been so stupid.

I called Ruth to tell her to come pick me up. We were going for a drive.

"Where?" she wanted to know.

"Pilkin's Knob."

"Why?"

I told her.

"I'll be right there."

I paced the office while I waited for her. Now I knew how Ruth felt when she waited for her ride to take her bowling. Pacing didn't help any, but it was better than just sitting there.

"What brought all of this on?" Ruth asked as I climbed into her yellow Volkswagen beetle.

"Nothing brought it on," I said. "I wasn't even thinking about Amel Pilkin at the time. I was planning to call you to tell you that I'd be working late and wouldn't be home for supper when I saw Clyde Beaman drive by. Then it hit me. What if Amel really had been carrying a letter in that envelope the night he died, and what if he mailed it to himself before he left for home. That would explain why no one ever found it."

"So you think it's been sitting there in his mailbox the whole time?"

"There's always that possibility, Ruth."

The Volkswagen hadn't even come to a complete stop when I jumped out and ran to Amel's mailbox. Inside it were a stack of letters and the last two editions of the *Oakalla Reporter*. But when I hurriedly looked through the letters, I saw that they were all junk mail.

"Damn," I said loudly enough for Ruth to hear.

"It was a long shot anyway," she said when I got back inside the Volkswagen. "You can't be too disappointed."

"But it all made sense," I complained, as if sense were enough to make it so. "And look at this," I said, showing her the stack of mail. "It's all here. Everything for the past three weeks. So nobody else thought to look in there."

"Unless he looked in, took what he wanted, and left the rest."

"That wasn't what I wanted to hear from you, Ruth."

I dropped the stack of mail on the back seat of the Volkswagen and told myself that I was through beating a dead horse. Whatever truths, or untruths, that Amel Pilkin had died with him. So be it. It was time to get on with my own life.

Ruth let me off at my office. I went back to work, finishing about ten before starting home. It was a clear and calm night, just as the day had been. I smiled at the irony of it all. Had Rupert Roberts still been sheriff, had Amel Pilkin not been deaf, had it been June instead of November, none of this would ever have happened. And had the dog not stopped to take a leak, he would've caught the rabbit.

"Ben Bryan called" was the first thing that Ruth said to me when I walked in the front door. "He wants you to call him back."

I was surprised to find her up since the stairway light was the only light on in the house. "At this hour?" I said.

She shrugged. "It's up to you. But if I were you, I would."

I studied her. She had something up her sleeve. Otherwise, she would have been watching the news, instead of sitting there in the near dark.

"Do you know what Ben's phone call is about?" I said.

"No. But I'd like to find out."

I called Ben Bryan, who answered after the third ring. "This is Garth," I said. "Ruth said you wanted me to call."

"There was no rush," he said. "Didn't Ruth tell you that?"

"No, she didn't," I said, feeling let down. "But go ahead anyway."

"Well, thanks to the spell of good weather that we've had lately, Danny Palmer finally managed to get that van dragged out of Hidden Quarry. Luckily, it had hung up on a shelf of rock and hadn't gone all the way to the bottom, or it would still be there. Anyway, Amel Pilkin was inside just like you said he'd be, and no worse for wear, I might add, since the water in the quarry was so cold."

"And?" I said, wondering where all of this was leading.

"And I checked him for cocaine, which I hadn't done before, and came up empty. So whatever he was babbling on to you about, it wasn't because he was high on cocaine."

"Damn," I said for the second time that day.

"Wasn't that the answer you wanted?"

"Two weeks ago it was. Not today. Today I'm ready to be done with Amel Pilkin and to get on with my own life."

"Welcome to the crowd," he said. Then he hung up.

"Ben didn't find any cocaine in Amel," I said to Ruth, as I sat down on the couch. "That's all he wanted."

She didn't look as disappointed as she should have. "I'm not surprised that he didn't," she said. "Look through Amel's mail again, and you might find out why."

I looked through Amel's mail again, but more slowly this time. Along with the two past issues of the *Oakalla Reporter* and the stack of junk mail was a yellow slip from the post office that said that Amel had a letter there with nine cents postage due on it.

"Why didn't I see that the first time?" I said, holding up the slip.

"Because you were looking for something else. But that's not all," she said. "Take a look at those two issues of the *Oakalla Reporter*. They're for last week and the week before that, but not for the day that Amel died. Which means that Amel probably did go home after he left the Corner Bar and Grill, just like Orville Goodnight said he did, and picked up the *Oakalla Reporter* on his way into the house."

"Which means what?" My brain had suddenly stopped working.

"It could mean that someone was there on Pilkin's Knob, waiting for him."

"Not Whitey Huffer," I said.

"No," she agreed. "Not Whitey Huffer. Not if he didn't recognize that jacket you were wearing the night you fought him."

"There's just one problem," I said. "Tomorrow is Thanksgiving. The post office will be closed."

Ruth smiled her "cat that ate the canary" smile. "Leave that problem to me."

27

AT DAYBREAK MAXINE Beaver, the postmistress, met Ruth and me at the back door of the post office. Maxine Beaver had been the postmistress of Oakalla ever since I could remember, which meant that she had been on the job at least thirty-five years, perhaps forty. It also meant that she was an old-school Oakallan, just like Ruth, and that, along with the fact that she and Ruth were also cousins, was what got us into the post office on Thanksgiving day.

"Don't you breathe a word of this to anyone," Maxine Beaver said. "Or I might lose my job."

"The day you lose your job," Ruth said with certainty, "is the day they put you out to pasture. Not before."

We went into the back of the post office where the outgoing mail was sorted and bagged for delivery. Most of the incoming mail would be sorted and put into one of the boxes there in the lobby, since we had no in-town delivery. The rest would be delivered by either Clyde Beaman or Shorty Harshbarger.

I handed Maxine Beaver the yellow slip that had been in Amel Pilkin's mailbox. It was delivered on the same Saturday that Amel had been found dead along Bear Hollow Road.

"I remember that letter," Maxine Beaver said. "It was addressed to Amel Pilkin, Oakalla, Wisconsin, but it had no return address, and only a twenty-cent stamp on it. Who would mail out a letter these days with only a twenty-cent stamp?"

That was what Ruth and I wanted to know.

We took the letter home and laid it on the kitchen table while Ruth put on a pot of coffee, and I sat watching her.

Someone had already opened the letter then taped it shut again. I guessed that Amel had opened it, read it, then taped it shut on his way through the hardware before he mailed it to himself. But where had he gotten the twenty-cent stamp to put on it?

I picked up the letter. "Do you want to do the honors?" I asked Ruth.

"No."

So I opened the letter, read it, then handed it to her. Meanwhile the coffee water boiled over onto the stove. I turned down the fire under the coffeepot and wiped off the stove.

"What do you think?" I asked when she finished.

"I don't know what to think, Garth, whether it's genuine or not."

"The letter's dated," I said. "It will be easy to check out to see if Warren Stout could have written it."

The letter read:

Dear Amel,

I am dying, and a dying man has a few privileges not accorded him in life. One of them is that he can speak his mind without fear of retribution. Another is that he can own up to all of his past sins and omissions without fear for the future.

You are both my sin and my omission. The sin came first. The omission later. Perhaps you will forgive me for both in time. Perhaps not. But that is your concern, not mine.

One snowy winter night some thirty years ago, I stayed too long at the Corner Bar and Grill and then had to find my way home. "Snow by then was everywhere. On the

ground and in the air, it was the sky above me and the
earth below. Everywhere was snow."

I slowed to a crawl to find my way along Bear Hollow
Road. It was then I saw your mother walking along in the
road in front of me. I didn't know her as your mother
then. I knew her as Lena Pilkin. In a few short hours, I
came to know her better.

I could blame what happened on the whiskey in me; or
on the unhappy fact that my wife was then seven months
pregnant with our second child and not inclined to warm
my bed that night, or any other night for that matter; or on
the special circumstances of that blustery night and the
unexpected delight in finding someone like your mother
to share it with me. But they would all be beside the
point. The truth is, I had had my eye on your mother for
a long time. She seemed such a simple and tender girl,
who would give her all and ask little in return. And I was
right. She was all those things and more.

So that night on Pilkin's Knob, under a patchwork quilt
on a straw mattress on the floor, I planted the seed that
was to become you, Amel. Thus, you are my son.

I am a wealthy man, Amel. I own nearly two thousand
acres of some of the richest farmland in Adams County.
A third of it is rightfully yours, if you choose to claim it.

But before you do claim it, let me plead my case. The
hardest thing I ever did, and my life has not been easy,
was to sell the land to get the money to give to your
mother to raise you. Not a day has gone by when I
haven't regretted my action. Not a day has gone by when
I haven't wished for that land back. The fact that your
mother spent the money changes nothing. It's the land for
which I grieve.

My two other children love their land as much as I.
They see it with the same eyes, hold it in the same
reverence, are owned by it as much as they are its owners.
And sometimes, no matter how much they love me, I
think they think I die too slowly.

Beware of them Amel. Beware of them . . . Wealth is

not life's only blessing any more than poverty is its only curse.

Sincerely,
Warren Sinclair Stout

"I think it's genuine," I said to Ruth. "Right down to the twenty-cent postage stamp."

"Then why wasn't it ever mailed?" She rose and poured us each a cup of coffee.

"Because Warren Stout probably gave it to Norman Fleischower with instructions to mail it as soon as Warren died. Only Norman Fleischower didn't mail it. He left it in his sport coat."

Ruth put a spoonful of sugar into her coffee, then handed the sugar bowl to me. "Why would he do that?" she said. "Just leave it in his sport coat?"

"He left it in there for fear of what might happen if he mailed it. True, he was Warren Stout's best friend. But he was also Warren's lawyer, and more than likely the one Warren sold the land to in order to get the money for Amel's mother. That was the way Norman got his farm, which has since become part of the Stout farm again. So rather than open a can of worms, Norman just kept the letter in his coat pocket and finally, just kept his coat in the closet. Carolyn Fleischower said he quit wearing it because her mother died. I wonder if he didn't quit wearing it so that he wouldn't have to face that letter every time he did."

Ruth took a drink of her coffee and grimaced. Evidently the coffee had perked too long. She took the half-and-half from me and added some to her coffee.

"Why didn't Norman Fleischower just burn that letter if he was so afraid of it?" she said. "I would have."

"Would you have?" I said. "What if I had written it and entrusted it to you? Would you risk me haunting you for the rest of your life by burning it?"

"I don't see how that would be much different than it is now," she said after tasting her coffee and reaching for the half-and-half again. "With all of your doings that somehow wind up in my lap. But your point is well taken. I probably wouldn't have burned it. I'd have probably put it away somewhere and let somebody in the future worry about it the way Norman Fleischower did."

"So would I. I think."

Ruth shook her head. "No, Garth. You would have mailed it. You and Aunt Emma and a few other people I know. That's the difference between you and me."

"It's not all that big a difference," I said.

She looked out the window at the gathering clouds. "Try to tell that to Whitey Huffer."

28

THE SNOW SQUALLS arrived as predicted just as Jessie and I turned onto Bear Hollow Road. At home Ruth had already put the turkey in the oven. I had left with the promise that I would be back by one and in time to eat it.

"What if you're not back by one?" she had asked.

"Then give Clarkie a call, and tell him where I've gone."

"What good will that do?" she had said.

I shrugged. I didn't have an answer for her.

I turned on Jessie's wipers to try to see where I was going. But it was snowing and blowing so hard that all the wipers did was grate my already jangled nerves. So I shut them off and tried to stay between the fence rows.

But by the time I reached Larry Stout's house, it had stopped snowing. The sun momentarily showed itself through a break in the clouds, and the wind, which came and went with the snow, barely blew at all. I shut off Jessie and sat there in the sun for a moment before I went to the door.

Buster Brown was inside the farmhouse with Larry Stout. He lay on a rug in the kitchen beside the wood stove that Larry was using to cook ham and beans. The small kitchen was warm and cozy with just enough room for the two of them. With me in there, it became crowded.

"What's on your mind, Garth?" Larry said, clearing a space at one end of the table for me to sit down.

Larry wore jeans, a green work shirt with both buttons off the sleeves, quilted underwear under his shirt, thick grey

179

wool socks, and no shoes. He had yet to shave that morning or to pick the snuff from between his teeth.

"You eating alone today?" I asked only because it was Thanksgiving.

"I eat alone every day," he said. "Unless I go into town and eat at the Corner Bar and Grill."

"What about Claire?"

"What about her?" he said, stirring the beans with a wooden spoon, then tasting them. He added salt and pepper.

"Where is she eating today?" I asked.

"Home, I guess. I never thought to ask her."

"You don't get together for Thanksgiving?"

He took another taste of the beans, then put the spoon down, and came to sit at the table. He sat at one end. I sat at the other. We seemed to balance each other out.

"No. We haven't gotten together for Thanksgiving since dad died," he said.

"Oh," I said.

"But you didn't come here to talk about Thanksgiving."

I unbuttoned my flannel shirt and took out Amel Pilkin's letter. "No," I said. "I came to show you this."

His cool grey eyes showed no interest in the letter. "I've seen it before," he said. "I haven't read it. But I've seen it. Where was it?"

"At the post office. Amel mailed it to himself."

"Clever of him."

"Yes, it was."

Buster Brown rose momentarily to scratch himself, then settled back down again. I could smell the ham and beans and onions cooking. They smelled good to me but not quite as good as the turkey and the oyster dressing that Ruth had been fixing at home.

"Just when did you see the letter?" I asked.

"Three weeks ago tomorrow," he said. "Amel came running up to me and started waving it in my face. Then he tried to hug me. But when Amel did that, Buster Brown stepped in between us and backed him off." He looked at

Buster Brown. "You weren't having none of that, were you, boy? You didn't bite him, but you sure came awful close."

Buster Brown raised his head and whined, then thumped his tail hard on the linoleum a couple times before stretching out on the floor again and closing his eyes.

"What happened then?" I said.

Larry took a can of Skoal from his shirt pocket and offered it to me. When I shook my head no, he took some for himself and put the can back into his pocket.

"Amel started jabbering at me so fast I couldn't understand him," he said. "Finally I threw up my hands in disgust and walked away from him." The look on Larry's face said that the worst was yet to come. "I'll never forget what happened next," he said. "Not if I forget everything else that's ever been said or done. *Brother*, he said to me as clear as a bell. You're my brother."

It grew so quiet in there that I could hear the ham and beans simmering on the stove. "You're sure that's what he said?"

"I'm sure. Because when I turned around to call him on it, he looked about as sad as I've ever seen a man look. And then a big tear came rolling down his cheek." Larry looked down at the table. I had never seen him so moved. "It was awful, Garth. The worst feeling I've ever felt in my life. I didn't know whether to hug Amel or to hit him."

"So which did you do?" I asked when he didn't continue.

"Neither one. Amel got into his truck and drove away. I just stood there and watched him go."

"And that was the end of it?"

He sat with his elbow on the table and his chin resting in his hand. There was a sad faraway look in his eyes, like that of a man who has dreamed the great dream but never dared to pursue it.

"I wish I would have let it end right there with Amel driving off into the sunset and me watching him go. It would have been a far happier day for all of us."

"But you went to Claire instead."

"Yes, I drove over to see Claire to ask her if it could be true. She said yes, that Dad had once confided in her that we had a half-brother running around Oakalla somewhere. He hadn't told me, she said, because he didn't know how I would take the news." He tried to smile. "It turned out that I was the least of his worries."

"What did Claire do when you told her?"

"Nothing. She said she had sows dropping pigs all over the place and couldn't worry about that now. But she said for me to find Whitey and see if we couldn't get that letter back. Either Dad or Norman Fleischower must have written it, she said. So it was probably official."

I looked down at Buster Brown who had started to snore. What a luxury it would have been to have lain down on the floor and joined him. "Which meant that it would be hard to sell that land to Bench-Mart once another heir entered the picture."

Larry looked down at Buster Brown and smiled. It seemed that he, too, would have liked to have curled up by the stove and been a dog for a day. "That was part of it," he said, "particularly for Whitey who needed the money from the sale of the land in the worst way. But for Claire, it was something more, I think. That letter threatened her whole way of life, or at least everything she had ever worked for. To give a third of it away to somebody else. Or worse, maybe have to sell the farm in order to divide it . . ." His eyes were keen and bright, right on the edge of tears. "Well, you'd just have to be a farmer to understand."

"I understand."

He shook his head sadly. "I'm glad someone does."

"You'd better stir the beans," I said. "It smells like they might be burning."

"Yeah, I guess I better."

He stirred the beans while I went to the window to look outside. The sky overhead was nearly all blue, but already I could see another squall building in the west.

"What's it doing out there?" Larry asked.

"Nothing at the moment."

"Give it time."

Yeah, I thought. Give it time.

Larry Stout sat down at his end of the table. I sat down at mine. Buster Brown continued to sleep by the stove.

"You were with Whitey the night Amel died?" I said.

"Yes," he said with regret. "I was with Whitey. We came into town and saw Amel's truck in front of the hardware. We thought we had Amel trapped in the Corner Bar and Grill because I was waiting outside one door and Whitey went in the other, thinking he would scare Amel out to me. But Amel must've seen us coming and beat it downstairs where we couldn't see him. So then when Whitey came out again, we drove around the block looking for Amel, thinking he might have doubled back on us. When we didn't see him anywhere, Whitey went back inside the Corner Bar and Grill to try to find him. The second Whitey stepped in the door, Amel popped up in the seat and took off in his pickup. I motioned for Whitey, and we started to give chase when a call came in on Whitey's radio, saying that the state police needed his backup on the interstate. So we had to give it to them." His face said what happened next was still a puzzle to him. "By the time we got back to Oakalla and tracked Amel down, he was already dead there along Bear Hollow Road. Whitey couldn't believe his good luck because it looked to us like Amel had broken down there, left his motor running, and died as a result. But when Whitey went to look for the letter, he couldn't find it, or anything else that had been in Amel's truck when it was parked there in front of the hardware. So he took the bottle of peach brandy out of Amel's glove compartment and dumped it all over Amel to make his death even more convincing. Then we went home to try to figure things out."

I had already been figuring things out. If not Whitey Huffer or Larry Stout, only one other person could have been waiting for Amel when he came home to Pilkin's Knob that night. And if I remembered right, as she had demonstrated when she killed a runt hog with a single blow to the head, Claire Huffer swung a mean hammer.

"And the night Whitey killed himself," I said. "He was here all along, wasn't he, until the call came from Claire that she had seen me take something from the dump behind their house."

"Yes, he was here," Larry said. "And swore on the phone to Claire that when he left here, he'd take care of you once and for all." Larry studied me, as he might a two-headed calf, or anything else that didn't fit into his straight-line view of things. "That's what I don't understand, Garth. You should be dead right now."

"When it came right down to it, Whitey couldn't pull the trigger," I said. "It was that simple."

"Claire can pull the trigger," he said solemnly, with a hint of brotherly pride.

29

THE CLOUDS CONTINUED to build in the west as I drove up the lane to Claire Huffer's house. It would snow again soon. I just hoped it didn't snow on me.

I knocked on the back door of the house. When Claire didn't answer my knock, I went inside to find her gone. On my way out the back door, I noticed the .22 Winchester carbine that usually hung above the door was also gone. I probably had Larry Stout to thank for that.

The .22 Winchester had an infrared scope on it, so that Claire could better see to shoot coyotes at night. If Claire was in the barn, where I now believed her to be, she with her infrared scope would have no trouble seeing me. And I knew from experience that whatever she could see to shoot at, she usually hit.

There were three ways into the barn that I knew of. One was through the big sliding doors on the west side. The two others were through the smaller swinging doors at either end of what was once the milking parlor. From the main floor of the barn, she could watch all three at once.

I didn't want to have to guess which door would be watched the closest. Once inside the barn without a weapon of my own, I would already be at her mercy; so even if I did surprise her and make it inside without getting shot, I'd have nowhere to go from there. My best plan was to leave and go for help.

But I didn't like that plan for two reasons. One, it would

make me look like a coward in Claire Huffer's eyes. Two, it would make me look like a coward in my own eyes. I could live with the first reason. I couldn't live with the second.

I climbed the gate and went out into the barnyard where the Holsteins were all huddled in the northeast corner, facing the wind. Then I felt a flake of snow brush my cheek and looked up to see several more drifting down. Then the wind began to rise and it began to snow harder. I turned up my collar and headed for the barn.

I had been in and out of enough barns to know that a lot of the older barns had an open area underneath them where the cows could go to get out of the weather. The opening under Claire Huffer's barn had been boarded up so that the cows could no longer get in, but by lying flat on my stomach face down in the dirt, I was able to squeeze through.

I then had to wait several seconds for my eyes to adjust to the dim light under there. While I waited, I listened. But I didn't hear anyone moving about in the barn above me.

To get to the main floor of the barn, I would have to climb up to it from the straw mow. To get to the straw mow was easy. All I had to do was to climb up and over a few boards. The hard part would be the climb out of the straw mow. Not hard in itself, but hard to do without getting shot.

I needed some ammunition and found it in the rock-hard corncobs that lay in the dirt all around me. After gathering as many as I could hold in my left hand, I scaled the boards and let myself down into the straw mow, then froze on the spot when I heard someone walking the main floor toward me.

Back over the boards I went, where I waited, crouched in the near darkness under the barn. Claire wouldn't give up her advantage, I didn't think, by going down there after me. Once again, she proved me wrong.

With a leap that I only heard, she landed in the straw mow, thrashed momentarily while she regained her feet, and started after me. I moved deeper under the barn where even the infrared scope would not be of much help to her. My right arm, which was my throwing arm, felt stiff and weak. I kept bending it up and down, up and down, to try to loosen it.

"Garth, I know you're under here," Claire said. She had climbed over the boards and was now there under the barn with me. "We don't have to have it end this way," she continued. "I can forgive everything that's happened, if you can."

I didn't say anything. Not that I doubted her sincerity, but I just wanted to make sure that she really meant what she'd said. So I tossed a corncob out away from me.

Twice the Winchester fired, once at the instant the corncob hit the ground and then the instant after that. She had to be shooting from the hip. She couldn't have aimed and fired that quickly.

I tossed out another corncob just to see what would happen. Twice more the Winchester fired. I tossed a third corncob and almost got shot for my trouble. Instead of firing at where it landed, she fired at me. The slug whirred by my ear and hit the foundation of the barn behind me. Another slug ripped through the space that I had just vacated the instant before she fired. Until you've been shot at in the dark, you can't really appreciate the flame a gun throws.

I lay in the dirt exactly where I'd landed after the first shot came at me. I was afraid to move for fear that she would zero in on me again. But I moved anyway because she had started walking toward me, firing twice as she came.

Scrambling on all fours, I slammed hard into the barn's foundation where I sat counting my teeth. Thirty-two. That meant I still had them all. Better yet, I was still conscious.

"Give it up, Garth," she said. "I know this barn too well. Already your back is to the wall." To prove her point, she fired, striking the foundation right above me.

I got up and moved at a right angle to her along the foundation, then stopped and planted my feet. For several minutes I had been warming up my right arm. The time had come to test it. "Claire."

She fired and once more hit the foundation, this time just inches away from me. I threw a corncob as hard as I could right at the spot where I thought her head would be, then charged after it.

She never knew what hit her. The corncob caught her squarely in the face as she was moving forward. She fired once into the ground and dropped the rifle. I was on top of her before she could recover.

"What did you hit me with?" she asked a few moments later.

She lay with her head in my lap. The rifle lay beside me well out of her reach. "A corncob," I said.

"I didn't know anyone could throw a corncob so hard."

"You're lucky. I once knocked a guy out with a baseball. He was wearing a helmet at the time."

"Lucky," she said.

A few minutes later, she rose to sit beside me, taking my arm in hers and resting her head on my shoulder. All in all, it wasn't too bad there under the barn out of the snow and the wind.

"What will happen to me now?" she said.

"I don't know. That's not up to me."

We sat in silence for a while. I reached down and felt in the dirt until I found the rifle. I wanted to make sure that it was next to me and not next to her.

"I intended to kill Amel," she said. "I intended it from the very beginning."

"Why don't you tell me what really did happen that night?"

She continued to stare off into the darkness. Then she sighed. I heard defeat in it and resignation.

"I was waiting for Amel when he came home that night," she began. "I stepped out of a shadow and hit him over the head before he even knew I was there. I hit him hard but not hard enough to kill him because he was still breathing when I turned him over to search him."

"And after that?" I said when she didn't continue.

"I searched his truck. Then I dragged him into it and drove him back here where I unloaded the barrels of trash so I could search through them later if need be. From there I drove him back to where they later found him. Searched him and his truck again, took the sport coat he was wearing off him, took the other sport coats piled on the seat of cab, loosened the universal joint, left the motor running, and came home."

"Why did you take the sport coat off of him," I asked, "when you'd already searched through it?"

"Because I couldn't stand the sight of seeing him in it." She spat the words at me as if they were too bitter to swallow. "Some of the happiest times of my life were when daddy, Norman, and I went somewhere, and Norman was wearing that sport coat. He was outrageous in it. But that was part of the charm, part of the fun of it all. The thought of Amel Pilkin wearing it, even in death, made me sick to my stomach."

"But it really wasn't his association with Norman Fleischower you objected to, or was it?"

"No, it was his association with daddy. I hated Amel Pilkin. I hated everything he was and everything he wasn't. I didn't want to share even daddy's memories with him."

"But Amel never even knew your father. At least not as father and son," I said.

"No," she said bitterly. "But daddy knew him. *Daddy*, I kept saying over and over to myself, how could you do this to me?"

"Would you like to read the letter?" I said. "It explains a lot."

Her head swung my way. I wished I could have seen into her eyes. It might have saved us both.

"Do you have it on you?" she asked.

I tapped my chest. "Inside my shirt."

She stiffened and sat apart from me. "No," she said. "I don't want to read it."

"Then are you ready to go?"

"Where?"

"Jail, I imagine. For now."

"What will become of the farm?" She couldn't hide the fear in her voice.

"I'd say that's up to you and Larry."

"I mean the everyday running of it. Larry has always left that up to me. I'm not sure he's capable of it."

"Then it will probably go under," I said, not trying to be kind.

"Divided three ways, it would have gone under anyway," she said sadly. "So what was I to do? You tell me, Garth. What was I to do?"

"I don't know, Claire. But killing Amel wasn't the answer."

She grabbed a handful of dirt and threw it hard at the opening under the barn. "God damn that Whitey," she said. "I wouldn't be in this mess, if it weren't for him. He had everything. He had me, the farm, even my best friend on the side. Why did he have to go and ruin it all with his gambling?" She pounded the ground with her fists. "Why? Why? Why?"

Her anger, though sincere, was hollow. She would have killed Amel Pilkin in any case, whether in debt or not. In truth, she didn't care what happened to Whitey Huffer, Amel Pilkin, or me. All she really cared about was her farm and its legacy.

I rose to my feet, taking the rifle with me. "Let's go, Claire."

"I'm not going," she said. "I'm not leaving this place in Larry's hands."

"You no longer have a choice."

"Sure I do. We always have a choice, Garth. We may not like it, but we always have a choice." Though the light was dim, I thought I saw her smile. "I'm quoting you on that."

"I don't ever remember writing that."

"You wrote it several years ago. When you were just starting out. I took it to heart."

"That long ago," I said.

"Yes," she said, her voice soft and sad. "That long ago."

"So what's your choice?" I asked.

"That rifle you're holding. That's my choice."

"That's not much of a choice," I said.

"It's better than the alternative. Or would you rather I go to prison for the rest of my life?"

"You don't know that will happen."

"You can't say that it won't. Please, Garth. I'm begging you. Just leave me the rifle and a couple shells in it. In case one isn't enough to do the job."

"I'm not sure I can do that, Claire. I don't want to have you on my conscience for the rest of my life."

"You're going to have me on your conscience regardless of what you do. This way at least, you will know I have forgiven you."

"Like you did before you started shooting at me?"

"I wasn't trying to hit you, Garth. I could have if I wanted to at any time I wanted to. You know that."

I didn't know that. But I didn't not know that, either. By my count there were at least two shells left in the rifle. Maybe three. But two should be enough.

"I still don't know, Claire."

"It's not your life, Garth," she pleaded. "It's mine. If you still feel anything for me at all, you'll give me this choice. It's the least you can do. Unless you want to shoot me yourself?"

"You know better."

"Then let me do it." She laughed. "At this range, how could I miss?"

I thought long and hard about it and decided that I owed her the choice. If I were in her shoes, I would want a choice, no matter how terrible that choice might be.

I carried the rifle with me as far as the opening where I

laid it down before sliding under the boards and outside. Then I began to walk quickly through the driving snow toward the gate and the barnyard beyond. I didn't want to hear the shot when it came. But I heard it anyway—at exactly the same time I felt the slug hit me just under my right shoulder.

I began to run, catching a board high on the gate with my right foot and springing on over. Once inside Jessie, I was relieved to see that I'd left the keys in the ignition. But then Jessie wouldn't start. She'd sputter, as if she truly intended to start, but I knew better. I opened my door and rolled out, as Jessie took a slug intended for me. Under the circumstances, I thought that only right.

As I ran up the lane into the wind and snow, I felt the whole time that I was losing ground. Adrenaline had set me on my way and kept me going for a while, but already I felt my legs start to go. The wind took its toll. So did the snow and the cold. But the slug in my back took the greatest toll.

I could feel my lifeblood draining out of me—along my spine and down the inside of my right leg. That was the warmest part of me. The rest of me began to feel cold and distant, as if it had no stake in this at all.

Then I began to imagine things. I imagined the snow suddenly ended, the sun peeped out, and standing there in the lane ahead of me was my guardian angel, looking for all the world like Rupert Roberts. If I can just reach him, I thought, I'll be saved.

But I never made it. My legs gave out and I fell. Unable to get up, or even to summon will enough to care whether I got up, I managed only to roll over on my back and stare up at a blue patch of sky while I waited for Claire Huffer to arrive.

She came surprisingly soon. But then she wasn't carrying a slug as I was. Looking up at her as she looked down at me, I thought I saw tears in her eyes—probably from the wind. Then she pointed the rifle at me.

30

THE FIRST THING I saw when I awakened was Ruth, sitting in a chair a few feet away. "This can't be heaven," I said.

"What makes you think you'd ever get that far?" She rose, bringing her chair with her, to sit beside my bed.

"How was the turkey?" I asked.

"What turkey?"

"Thanksgiving turkey."

She frowned. "Probably burned to a crisp by now. I forgot to shut the oven off."

"That's okay," I said. "I'm not hungry anyway."

She patted my pillow. "That makes two of us."

I lay there for a while, staring at the ceiling. I guessed I was in the hospital. It looked like a hospital ceiling to me.

"How come I'm here and not dead?" I said.

"You can thank Clarkie for that."

"He came to my rescue?"

She didn't say anything.

"So you called him after all," I said.

"Against my better judgment." She held up her thumb and forefinger to show me. "I came that close, Garth, to not calling him at all."

You couldn't have put a cat's whisker between her thumb and forefinger.

"None of us are perfect."

"Amen to that."

I stared at the ceiling some more. I had a question for her, but it could wait.

"Am I expected to live?" I asked.

"The last I heard anyway. The bullet just nicked your lung. You lost a lot of blood, but that was the worst of it. Doc Airhart says you'll be up and out of here in no time."

"Doc Airhart?" I said. "What was he doing here?"

She didn't want to tell, but she couldn't find any way around it. "The surgeon was busy with another patient. So they called in Doc to work on you."

"How is the other patient?" I asked, which was the question that I'd kept waiting.

"I'm sorry, Garth. But she died on the operating table."

I closed my eyes, then opened them when I felt in control again. "I guess it's better than prison," I said.

"Let's hope so anyway." She rose from the chair and put on her coat and scarf.

"Where are you going?"

"Cecil Edwards and I have a newspaper to put out."

"You mean it's still Thursday?"

She pulled up her coat sleeve to look at her watch. "For several more hours yet," she said. "It's just going on six now."

"Somehow it seemed later." When she was almost to the door, I said, "Ruth, where's Clarkie? I'd like to thank him if he's around."

She shook her head in puzzlement. "He's nowhere to be found, Garth. Not once he got the word about Claire Huffer."

"Can you blame him?"

"No. I can't say that I do." She shouldered her purse and left.

For the next couple hours, I dozed on and off and lay there stupefied the rest of the time. My mind had no sharp edges to it, no sight and no focus. For once in my life, I didn't want to think about anything.

Carolyn Fleischower came into the room and took the

seat that Ruth had left. She wore a long brown tweed coat, a red scarf, and a small brown pillbox hat. Her eyes were big and bright, and her cheeks were rosy from the cold.

"Are you okay?" she asked softly.

I turned to look at her. "I'm okay."

She sat stiffly with her hands folded in her lap, perhaps to help hold her together. "So how do I say I'm sorry?"

"To Claire or me?"

"To either one of you."

"Simple is best." I reached out and took her hand in mine. "But I don't need an apology. I don't think Claire needs one, either."

She was trying hard to keep from crying. "But I knew, Garth," she said. "I knew all the time what everyone was after. At least I knew once Whitey told me."

"So did some other people," I said. "None of them stepped forth, either."

"Claire was my best friend," she said.

"I know."

She took my hand in both of hers and started to sob. I avoided it as long as I could. Then I did something I hadn't done since Grandmother Ryland died. I broke down and cried.

31

LATE THE NEXT afternoon, I was released from the hospital, and Ruth drove me home under a pink and purple sky. Home had never looked so good to me. I didn't kneel down and kiss the threshold, but I felt like it.

Ruth and I ate an early breakfast the next morning and were about to leave for Madison in her Volkswagen when Clarkie came to the door. I invited him in.

"I can't stay long, Garth," he said, taking off his sheriff's hat and holding it in both hands against his chest. "I just came by to see how you're doing."

"Why don't you have a seat," I said. "I can't stand up for long."

Clarkie looked first at me and then at Ruth as if he weren't sure that he'd be welcome. Finally he sat down on the couch, but right on the edge of the cushion with both feet directly under him, like a first-time suitor. I sat down beside him, while Ruth found something she needed to do upstairs.

"So," he said after a long pause. "How are you doing?"

"Fine, thanks to you. In fact, Ruth and I are just about to leave for Madison."

"Is that wise?" he asked.

"Probably not." Particularly in light of where we were headed.

"I mean," Clarkie continued, "the last time I saw you, I didn't know if you were ever going anywhere again."

"The last time I saw you, I thought you were Rupert

196

Roberts," I said. "That was you, wasn't it, standing at the end of Claire Huffer's lane?"

"That was me," he said, not wanting to talk about it. "I saw you running toward me and got out of my patrol car to see what was going on."

"Thanks, Clarkie. I owe you my life."

He looked down at the floor and didn't say anything.

"She was going to kill me, Clarkie," I said. "You know it and I know it."

It seemed to take all of his willpower to raise his head to look at me, but he did it. "The rifle was empty, Garth."

"You didn't know that. Neither did she."

"I didn't know that," he agreed. "But I'm not so sure about her." He quit his perch on the edge of the couch and sank back against the cushion. "It never ends, Garth," he said. "I do the right thing for once and end up killing a woman holding an unloaded gun. Can you imagine what the folks around here are going to say now?"

I was going to leap to his defense, but he never gave me the chance.

"The thing is, Garth, I don't care anymore what the people of Oakalla say. I was the one out there on the firing line. Not them. And I acted like Rupert Roberts or any other lawman worth his salt would have acted. I saw what needed to be done and did it. I'm not proud of how it turned out, but I'm not ashamed either."

"Good for you, Clarkie," I said.

"You mean you're not mad at me?" He still acted as if he thought I should be.

"For what, Clarkie?"

"Killing Claire Huffer. You two were close, or at least that's the impression I got."

Clarkie sank deeper into the couch. He set his hat on the cushion beside him.

"It's true," I said. "Claire and I were close. But that didn't stop her from trying to kill me."

He nodded as if he understood.

A few seconds later, he rose from the couch. I went with him as far as the front door. "Does this mean you're staying on as sheriff?" I asked.

"For the time being, anyway," he said. He stepped outside, then turned back to me. "I almost forgot. Jessie's up at the Marathon. Danny said you can pick her up anytime."

"How about next spring?"

Clarkie smiled. "Danny said you'd say something like that."

Moments later Ruth and I left for Madison. The heater on her Volkswagen worked about as well as Jessie's heater, and by the time we pulled into the First Fidelity Union parking lot, I could hardly feel my toes.

"You going to make it all right?" Ruth asked.

"I think so. But follow me as far as the lobby just to make sure."

Once inside the bank, I opened the first oak door on the right and climbed the oak stairs to Lincoln Thomas' office. In some ways Lincoln Thomas resembled a frog with his bald head, bulbous eyes, and thick jowls, and the way he sat, eyes closed, apparently drowsing, in his swivel chair, like a fat green frog on his lily pad. But appearances could be dangerous as well as deceiving, as the foolish fly found out when he flew too close to the frog. I doubted that Lincoln Thomas ever drowsed, either in his swivel chair or in his business dealings.

"So we meet again, Mr. Ryland," he said.

Only his mouth moved. The rest of him still sat there in repose. But I could now barely see the pupils of his eyes.

"You mind if I have a seat," I said, sitting down. "I just got out of the hospital."

"Hernia?" he said in an apparent attempt at humor.

"Gunshot wound."

His eyes opened a little wider. "Who shot you?"

"Claire Huffer."

"And she is?"

"Dead."

His eyes were wide open now. They were cold and blue and bloodshot, like the sunrise that morning. "That does present a problem then," he said.

"I thought it might. But I did bring along some of Whitey's old gambling markers, in case you were still in the market."

He leaned across his desk toward me. He was so large and intimidating, it was easy to see why Whitey Huffer had referred to him as the Big Man. Had I owed him two hundred thousand dollars, I would have thought of him as the Big Man, too.

"What is it you want, Mr. Ryland? If it's blackmail money, I'm afraid you'll have to get in line."

I heard the oak door open and close and then somebody start up the stairs. I didn't think it was Ruth. My guess was it was the security guard, who likely moonlighted as Lincoln Thomas' driver.

"Are you okay, Mr. Thomas?" I heard him say.

"I'm okay, Franklin. But I'm afraid you're going to have to show Mr. Ryland out."

"Over my dead body," I heard Ruth say from the bottom of the stairs.

I smiled at Lincoln Thomas. He didn't smile back. "Looks like a Mexican standoff to me," I said.

Lincoln Thomas sat perfectly still for a few seconds, then said, "Thanks, Franklin. That will be all for now."

"Are you sure, Mr. Thomas?" Franklin sounded as if he wanted a piece of me.

"Yes, Franklin, I'm sure."

Franklin went back down the stairs. I heard the oak door close behind him.

"I repeat, Mr. Ryland, if it's money you want, you'll have to get in line."

"Don't tell me you're running short? I didn't think that ever happened to loan sharks."

He shrugged. "Hard times come to all of us at one time or another, and this appears to be my time."

"Then you admit you are a loan shark? That you bought up all of Whitey Huffer's gambling markers so that he would be in debt to only you? And then helped engineer the sale of Claire Huffer's land to Bench-Mart to be sure you got your money?"

He didn't deny it. He didn't seem to think it was necessary. "If you insist," he said.

"So what was Claire Huffer's money supposed to buy you, some breathing room or some traveling money?"

He again took his time in answering. He didn't trust me any further than I trusted him. "It all depended on how things fell."

"So what are you going to do now?"

"Wait."

"For what?"

Lincoln Thomas smiled for the first time. I didn't like his smile. It was far too sure of itself.

"Whatever comes along," he said. "If life has taught me anything, it is patience. You wait, wait, and then wait some more. Only the very few have the heart to endure to the end." His smile sharpened. "I have nothing to fear from the rest."

"One of the things that won't come along," I said, "is the money Whitey Huffer owed you. That's why I'm here today, to tell you that debt is paid."

"Claire Huffer has a brother, if I remember right," he said, "who should now own all of the Stout farm."

"Lean on him," I said, "and I'll lean twice as hard on you."

"With what?" If my threat had scared him any, he didn't show it.

"My newspaper for one thing. My syndicated column for another. There's not a town in this area that doesn't read it. That includes Madison."

"I could make things very difficult for you," he said.

I rose. My chest had started to hurt, but I didn't want him to know that. "Likewise, I'm sure."

I started for the stairs. But Lincoln Thomas wasn't

through with me yet. "Ryland," he said, "you took a hell of a chance coming here. Particularly the first time when things could have gone either way."

"Maybe," I said. "But that's not how I saw it."

"How did you see it then?"

I took a moment to think about it. Up until then, I hadn't tried to put my thoughts on the subject into words. "Let's just say I'm a duck, who no matter how hard he falls, always lands on his feet."

"And the one time you don't land on your feet?"

I smiled. He'd walked right into it. "I'm a dead duck."

His look said that he would wait for that day.

"I have a question for you," I said. "And it's off the record."

"Then I might answer it," he replied.

"Why did you help Whitey Huffer steal Amel Pilkin's body?" I asked. "Were you afraid that the Bench-Mart deal might fall through if it were discovered that Amel Pilkin had been murdered?"

"Whitey was, though I don't think that was his main concern."

"What was his main concern?" I asked, though I thought that I already knew the answer. It was the same reason that helped drive Whitey to suicide.

"His wife was his main concern," Thomas answered. "He was afraid she might have killed Amel Pilkin, but without a body, you see, no one could ever prove it."

"And without a body, you still might get your two hundred thousand dollars."

He smiled ever so faintly. "There was always that chance."

"Ever the optimist," I said. He didn't see the irony, or if he did, he didn't acknowledge it.

"In this business you have to be."

"Satisfied?" Ruth asked as she stared the Volkswagen.

"I don't know, Ruth," I said. "Claire Huffer, Whitey

Huffer, and Amel Pilkin all end up dead, and what does Lincoln Thomas get? Maybe this week he'll have to eat pork chops instead of prime rib at the country club, but that's about it. It's the same old story. The Big Man takes the money and walks. The little guy takes the fall."

"So how do you propose to change things?" she said.

"Ask me tomorrow. I'll be a day smarter."

On our way out of the bank parking lot, we passed Lincoln Thomas' grey Mercedes convertible parked in the space reserved for the bank president. "Wait a minute, Ruth," I said.

After she'd stopped the Volkswagen, I shut it off and took the key out of the ignition. Then, starting at the front fender, I ran the key all the way along the left side of Lincoln Thomas' Mercedes. It was a stupid and childish thing to do, but it gave me great pleasure.

"Now I'm satisfied," I said to Ruth, handing her the key.

She gave me a harsh look that I took for disapproval.

"And don't ask me to explain myself, either."

She started the Volkswagen and drove on. "I was just wondering," she said, "why you didn't do the other side while you were at it."

We drove to University Hospital, where after asking twice for directions, I finally got to where I was supposed to be. I was standing at the desk when Dr. Byron Winters hurried by. He stopped, did a double take, and returned to the desk.

"Mr. Ryland," he said, surprised, yet pleased, to see me. "I really wasn't sure you'd show up today."

"I really wasn't sure I'd show up, either."

"Do you still want to go through with it?"

While lying in my hospital bed, I'd had a long time to think about it. I never again would be able to father a child. But then, in the final analysis, did I really want to?

"That's what we need to talk about," I said.

"Then follow me."